AMONG SHADOWS

A COLOR ALCHEMIST NOVELLA

NINA WALKER

ADDISON & GRAY PRESS

Ebook ISBN: 978-1-950093-10-6

Paperback ISBN: 978-1-950093-11-3

This is a prequel novella
to The Color Alchemist series.

I dedicate this book to the aspiring authors out there.
Keep writing.

ONE

I hissed, catching sight of my face in the mirror. The bruise was already blossoming along the bone. "He's home tonight," I grumbled. "Just great." Talk about crappy timing.

Some fights were far more dangerous than the physical damage done. Sure, cuts and bruises weren't fun, but it was staying home from school that was the problem. It would be noted on my record. It wasn't the first time. But going to school and facing my peers with a busted-up face? That was far worse. Every time I came home with a new injury, Mom would insist on keeping me locked up safe and sound at home. She said that if evidence of fighting happened enough times, I'd be questioned by the police, and that could lead to something worse, something my parents refused to talk about.

Troublemakers weren't welcome in New Colony society. Even I knew that.

I tensed as I skulked down the stairs for dinner, my footsteps a soft thud on each carpeted step. The spicy rich aroma of Mom's cooking set my stomach rumbling. I just hoped her food wouldn't cause any arguments from Dad. She rarely made the Asian cuisine passed down from her mother and grandmother anymore. Dad didn't like it, said it wasn't patriotic and that if she were found out, he wasn't going to defend her. Prick.

I had to be more careful. When I fought, I rarely walked away with any visible evidence. But things had taken an ugly turn earlier, and since Dad was home tonight, I'd have to deal with the oncoming lecture. I hated when he was home. He traveled around the kingdom so much that most days he was away on business, leaving Mom and I to our peace.

"What happened this time?" His heavy glare caused my step to falter, but only for a second. I could always count on Mom not to overlook the fighting, but he always had something negative to say. His blatant hypocrisy drove me mad. And anyway, it wasn't always pointless fighting; it was usually boxing, which used to be an admirable sport before it lost sanction.

I shook my head. "It's not what you think."

Mom glanced over a mountain of steaming rice as she set the bowl on the dining table. She paused for a second, blinked back tears, and then forced a small smile. Shame grasped at my throat, choking me. Suddenly, I wasn't all that hungry anymore.

"Sit down, honey," she said calmly.

Silence stretched the moment taut as a wire as I slid into the wing-backed chair. Our dining room was much nicer than most, and Mom took great pride in keeping the dark wood furniture and floors polished to perfection. Ours was a house full of rooms, sometimes full of highly ranked people, but as for the family inside, we were practically ghosts.

"You always do this, Cathy." Dad turned his heavy glare on Mom, and she immediately shrank in her seat. She didn't respond. She never did when he was like this. She was a physically small woman who'd been trained her whole life to be even smaller. I got my Asian features from her, since her ancestry was Chinese, and I was proud of that, but even that heritage had been snuffed out of her over time. Except for the food, of course. She still made incredible Chinese meals, insisting upon it. Tonight was no different. The food made my mouth water and I eyed a perfectly constructed dumpling before plopping it onto my mouth. Screw this conversation; my appetite was back and I wasn't about to let perfectly good food go to waste.

"Stop sticking your head in the sand and

pretending the boy is fine." Dad waved a finger to the cut on my lip and the purple bruise right above it. "Clearly, he is not okay. This is not okay."

I chuckled. "Why? Because people can see this one?"

Mom dropped her fork onto her plate with a noisy clatter. "Don't talk to your father that way," she whispered.

"What did you just say to me?" Dad shifted in his seat, carefully removing his cloth napkin from his lap and setting it on the table. He adjusted his black silk tie and rolled his shoulders back with a pop. He was the picture of a perfect court dignitary, and he fit in with the majority of New Colony's citizens: clean-cut and obedient.

"Todd, please," Mom whispered, her smile faltering yet again. "Let's just enjoy our dinner. Tristan didn't mean it."

Oh, but I did mean it.

Dad's eyes stayed fixed on mine, pinning me to my chair. I held the stare, equally ready to fight back. Blood rushed through my head like water running over my ears, but I held my focus. I wasn't afraid of him anymore, and from the way his chest puffed up and his eyes narrowed, I think he knew it.

Finally, he nodded. "Fine. I'll deal with you after dinner."

Mom didn't respond. That was fine. I'd decided long ago that I'd rather take the brunt of his rage. I was nearly seventeen, and I could handle myself. I'd grown tall over the last couple of years, muscles growing as I obsessed over my training, exercising and fighting. Having a way to protect myself had become my religion, and I worshiped daily.

Dad hated it.

But he couldn't control me anymore, and as much as I loved my mother, she'd given up long ago. She was just an extension of him now, except during these meals, which he always hated but she loved. Meat and potatoes, he'd say, that's the New Colony way.

As we ate in silence, I shoveled as many of the juicy pork dumplings and all the mounds of sticky rice into my mouth that I could handle. If I was going to be skipping school for a few days, as was always the case after I got hit in the face, I'd be stuck at home. And considering the unfortunate fact that Dad was home tonight, he'd be putting a lock on the fridge and cabinets that he wouldn't remove until he got home tomorrow night. It was his most recent form of punishment now that I was bigger than him. And it would be doubly effective, reminding Mom that he didn't appreciate her Asian cuisine, and reminding me to stay in line. I glared at the food on the table, continuing to eat and eat and eat. I had to fill up while I could.

"Thanks, Mommy." I smiled over the fork between my lips. "Delicious as always. I sure do appreciate when you bring this ethnic flair into our home."

She looked away, the three of us shocked by my words. But truth was, I meant it. We shouldn't have to wash our ancestry away just to make Dad feel more comfortable. He married Mom, after all. What did he expect?

Just as I scraped the last of my food off my porcelain plate and into my mouth, Dad snapped. "You know what, Tristan? I'm sick of this." He sat his fork carefully on his dish with a light clang and relaxed into his chair, smoothing a wrinkle on his shirt. He appeared calm on the outside, but I wasn't fooled. Something was coming.

"You're always getting into fights," he continued, his voice cold as midnight in winter, "and your mother and I are stuck trying to protect you from the consequences."

I swallowed my food and took my time drinking a long gulp of water, letting out a deep sigh of satisfaction. "What's your point, Dad?"

His body hardened as he rolled back his shoulders and grit his teeth. "My point is, enough is enough. No more missing school. No more hiding your indiscretions."

The tension in the room felt like a balloon about to pop.

"No," Mom burst out, "you can't!"

Dad slammed his palms down onto the table, his head whipping in her direction, his glare hard.

"You know what they do to the kids who get into fights," she explained weakly, all challenge in her voice falling away. Then her face tilted down and her body fell into its familiar obedient pose.

"Maybe it's time Tristan faced the consequences of his actions and learned a lesson about the way life works around here," Dad said, eyes on her. He stood, his chair scratching against the hardwood as he pushed his plate away with a clatter. Tears welled in Mom's eyes, but she put her fork down and pushed her plate away as well. Neither had touched much of their food.

The message was clear. He didn't appreciate her working hard on creating meals outside of what was socially acceptable by his peers. It wasn't the first time he'd been upset about it, nor the first time he'd refused the food, but it was the first time she'd stopped eating it herself. Anger welled up inside me. Why did he have to be so unkind to her about it? There weren't any rules against her Asian cooking. She wasn't breaking any laws.

"Thank you for cooking this food, Mom," I said, licking my lips. "It was incredible."

Dad's dark eyes narrowed into slits as he eyed me with outright disdain. My body tensed, ready to spring into action should I need to defend myself. Given enough coaxing, he would hit me, and today, I would welcome it.

"You'll not be missing one more day of school, no matter how many bruises show up on that pathetic face of yours." Then he stormed from the room, knocking over his chair with a thunk and leaving Mom to stew.

I sighed. Maybe he wouldn't be "dealing with me" after all. Perhaps this was his way to punish me, just make me face the ridicule at school. Lately he'd noticed how big I was getting; I saw it in his eyes, his indignation. I was bigger than him and he hated it. I saw the way he studied me, staring at my biceps with a hateful curl of his lip. Next time he felt like taking a swing at me, if I fought back, I'd probably win. And we *both* knew it.

"I'm so sick of this house," I grumbled, getting up as well. I, however, knew how to control myself, so no chairs were harmed.

"I'm sorry," Mom said softly, but she didn't look at me. Her hair hung around her narrow shoulders in a perfect sheen of silky black.

My breath released through my nostrils and I shook my head at Mom, an ache clenching my heart. I didn't understand her sometimes, but I wasn't mad at her either. She was forced to deal with him same as I was. It wasn't her fault he was abusive. I'd never seen him lay a finger on her, but that didn't stop him controlling her in almost every way. She went right along with it for the most part. When love and fear mixed, I guess that's what people like her did. Countless times I'd sworn I'd report him. Next time he hit me, I'd do something about it—that was always my thought. But then she'd beg me not to, and I always gave in. I shouldn't have.

Eventually, he would push me too far. Or worse—he'd hit her.

I strode around the table and draped my arms around her back, resting my chin on the top of her head. Her hair smelled of familiar sugar and vanilla, and I knew some extravagant baked goods probably waited in the kitchen. Though she cherished the recipes passed down from her mother and grand-mother, the act of baking more traditional New Colony treats relaxed her. She reached up and squeezed my arms.

"It'll be okay," I muttered.

She shook her head and sniffed, wiping away a loose tear. Guilt weighed heavy between us. Maybe it would be fine, maybe it wouldn't. But the fight I had earlier today? That wasn't my fault. Bryce had gone too far. No one was supposed to walk away with bruises on their face.

"Maybe Dad is right," I said as I unwrapped myself from Mom and began stacking the plates. "Maybe you should stop protecting me."

If I had to explain the bruises, I could always tell them about my father, say he was the culprit. Sure, he hadn't been the one to hit me this time, but he'd done it enough in the past that it wouldn't exactly be a lie.

"You don't mean that." She stood and squared her shoulders.

But the thing was, I did mean it. I was tired of living in this awful house the way we were. I was tired of Dad and his anger. It followed us around like a poisonous snake, always ready to strike. Maybe if I fought back, maybe if I shook things up a little, I'd free us from his venom.

I shot Mom my cheekiest grin, trying to lighten the mood. "Did you bake a cake?"

"Cookies," she sighed, a small smile slipping through her sadness.

I waggled my eyebrows. "Race you to the kitchen," I yelled out, darting around her and sprinting from the room, the stack of dishes, like my emotions, barely hanging on for balance.

TWO

"Well, look who decided to show his ugly face today," Bryce Chapmen sneered and laughed that horrible little laugh of his. I ignored the idiot and slid into my desk. The stares of thirty classmates fell on my back, heavy as lead. My bruised face only looked worse in the light of morning; my cheek was less of a cheek and more of a bruised plum. Not pretty and hard to miss.

A flicker of shame sparked deep inside, but I shut that crap down immediately.

It wasn't a secret to many of my classmates that I got into fights behind the school every now and again. The fights here were just a natural reaction to some jerk who deserved to be put in their place. Luckily with those, I'd yet to be caught by the administration.

No, it was the secret fights that happened after school that were beginning to show up in public. The ones in the warehouse. Those were my training. My necessary evil.

Stupid Bryce...

"Let's see if Daddy can help you this time." Bryce laughed, raking a hand through his greasy blonde hair as he slid into the desk behind mine.

The room was normally buzzing with conversation, but not today, not when Bryce and I were glaring each other down. Truth was, we all had important parents with pull to get us out of sticky situations. Anything Bryce said to me could be flung right back on him, not that his brain was intelligent enough to see his blatant hypocrisy.

"Or maybe Mommy couldn't protect you," he continued, running his mouth.

"You better shut up." I turned on him.

"Or what?"

He of all people should know better!

"Or you'll be sporting a black eye as well, and we can *both* deal with the consequences." My glare turned sharp, anger building. This whole thing was his fault. "You know what I'm capable of," I hissed, then cracked my knuckles and snarled my lip.

He studied me for a moment. His snarky gaze shifted to my fists, but he didn't respond. His tanned skin drained to white and he swallowed hard, eyes flicking away.

"That's what I thought," I growled, turning back to the front of the classroom.

Our instructor chose that moment to enter, impervious to our heated exchange. Edgemount Academy was the finest high school in the capital city, filled with the children of dignitaries, courtesans, and government officials, but that didn't change the fact that most of the people here were complete brown-nosing tools. Even the teachers.

Especially the teachers.

"All right students," Mr. Lansing said, running his mousy hands down his perfectly pressed brown suit, "please power on your slatebooks and let's get started on yesterday's homework."

I did as he said, keeping my head down. It wouldn't be long before he'd notice my bruised appearance. How would he react? Would he report me?

Probably.

But it seemed luck was on my side because Lansing only glanced at me, raised an eyebrow, and then turned away to continue his history lesson. *That's right, nothing to see here.* I followed along the best I could, a rising tide of anxiety threatening to pull me under. By the end of the lecture, I'd barely retained a word.

After class, I headed for mathematics, my backpack casually slung over one shoulder of the stupid preppy blazer I was forced to wear. I kept my head up, a smirk playing at my lips. Students jumped out of my way. *What? No one wanted to be associated with the screw-up today? Whatever.*

That was the problem. We weren't allowed to make mistakes. Because of that, we rarely did. And fighting? It wasn't just frowned upon, it was forbidden.

Illegal.

But I hardly ever did it at school or in public. I had a place to go, a secret place where I could fight others like me. Guys who wanted to know how to defend themselves. Or who enjoyed the sport of it. I only shuffled into that place when things reached breaking point. When I had to punch something or else I would be the one that broke.

"What's up with your face, man?" My oldest friend, Tyler, met me at the door of the classroom, and we took our seats next to each other. "You know you can't show that around here." He played it off cool, but I detected the worry in his tone. He wasn't the only one.

"Dear old Daddy's orders," I sighed. "Some crap about how I need to learn about consequences."

His smile faltered, eyes wide as saucers. "I'm sorry, but your dad's a real dick."

"You've met him," I replied with a scoff. "Don't look so surprised."

Tyler shook his head and shrugged. "Be careful, man."

"Hopefully the administration won't report anything." I swallowed. He nodded, letting out a resigned breath.

The rest of the day went about the same: teachers avoided eye contact, and students whispered behind my back. I ignored the occasional brazen comments. That was easy enough, but the fear that clung to me like a dark shadow was not. It lingered, trying to get through my hard exterior, reminding me of the truth. *You're not going to get away with this.*

Just because I went through the day and nothing happened, didn't mean it wouldn't be noted down and reported by someone to be dealt with later. Pushing things under the rug wasn't how things operated in New Colony. There would be a follow-up. Always. The best I could hope for was a warning. The worst? I didn't even want to think about it. And knowing my father, if I went down, I was going down alone.

THREE

I eyed the mangled building up ahead. It fit in with the others in the area. This whole neighborhood was a patchwork of desolation. Nondescript and rundown, it was one of many forgotten warehouses on the outskirts of town. Nearly everything in the capital city had a purpose. Most of the relics from the old America had been destroyed or refurbished to suit New Colony's needs. Plus, there'd been a massive amount of new construction in recent years. But there was a whole section of town to the northeast left by the wayside. I had to take two trains and then walk a quarter mile to get to it.

Loose gravel and a few bits of broken glass crunched under my boots as I approached the rusted metal door. With a quick look over my shoulder to make sure I was alone, that I wasn't being followed, I ducked into the dark doorway.

I was late ... but I'd made it.

The scent of salty sweat and dirt greeted me first. I blinked, my eyes adjusting to the darkened open space with a couple of spotlights in the center. I slipped out of my jacket and shoved it into my bag, dropping it on the pile with the others.

"Back for more?" Bryce's scratchy voice appeared from almost nowhere, far too close to my ear. I swear the kid was waiting for me, which meant he was waiting for me to knock his teeth out.

I rolled my shoulders and ignored him, walking away from where Bryce hid among the shadows and toward the circle of men. These were the guys I preferred to associate with, not Bryce. The fact that he had become a regular here in recent weeks was the biggest stain on this place. But still, the fights pulled me back again and again, an itch that needed to be scratched.

But I am not my father's son. Just because I like this stuff, doesn't mean I would ever take joy in hurting those too weak to fight back. It was a reminder I had to give myself often.

"Your face is still busted." Horace, the leader of the group, walked over. His frown was deep as he assessed the damage. "You shouldn't have left your house today, let alone come here."

Horace ran this place. He made the rules. But he didn't *really* know what my father was like, so taking the time to explain why I had been let out of the house seemed like a waste of breath. I only shrugged. Horace was short and wired tight with ropy muscle. A deep scar crossed over one eye, giving him a menacing look. But he was kind, and that was what brought me here in the first place. I'd hoped he take pity on me.

"Come back when you're healed," Horace's voice was sharp.

"Come on, what's a few more bruises?" I joked, but it fell flat. My hands had already formed into fists, and I'd inadvertently turned my gaze to Bryce. For all his wisecracks at school, he was the one who'd put this shiner on my face. More than anything, I wanted to repay the favor.

"I mean it," Horace pressed, his voice going low. "You shouldn't be here looking like this. There will be questions about that bruise if there weren't any already."

"If I have to go, Bryce has to go, " I challenged.

We all knew the rules. No hitting the face or anywhere that could leave visible marks in public, because that could be traced back to us. What we were doing here? Like I said, illegal. No one had any delusions about that. If the royal family or any of their cronies caught wind of this place, we'd all be screwed. But yesterday Bryce had gone too far, laying into my face the first chance he got. The men had jumped in and pulled us apart before I got the opportunity to pummel him back. I wasn't about to give up on delivering justice now that I was here with Bryce only a few yards away.

"Fine, you can stay and watch, but no fighting. Not with that injury," Horace huffed, shaking his head like he couldn't believe himself.

Bryce chuckled as he walked past. My glare hardened.

"You either, Bryce." Horace pointed a meaty finger between us. "I mean it. No fighting for either of you tonight."

Bryce shrugged as if he didn't care. I knew that was bull. He loved this place as much as I did. But we were different. I was here to learn how to defend myself. To protect my mom if I ever need to. Bryce wanted to hurt people. With the laws being what they were, he didn't have much of an opportunity to do that before he'd found this place and the men here, each of us carrying our own sad story.

Horace eyed us both closely until we gave in and nodded our agreement. The man was one of few words, but I knew better than to test him. I'd seen enough times what happened when people broke the rules. Horace was an animal among animals here. In this place, he was king. At least I didn't have to leave. Watching would have to be good enough for now.

I gave Bryce one last glare and then joined the sidelines to study the next match; maybe I'd learn a thing or two. If I was lucky, the crack of knuckle on bone would satiate my burning anger, my clawing need to fight tonight.

Two men stepped out into the middle of the circle. They were older guys, probably mid-forties, because they looked about my Dad's age, except these men held stories in their weathered skin. They sized each other up, and I could practically see the thoughts running through their heads. From the looks of them, one was clearly bigger and stronger. Chuck looked like a Neanderthal, so it would seem he had the upper hand. But I knew different. His opponent, Lee, was a force to be reckoned with. Lee was a tad scrawny, but he was fast. He sported lean, corded muscles that packed a killer punch. I'd been on the receiving end on more than one occasion.

Chuck dove in, grabbed Lee around the torso, and immediately tried to flatten him to the ground. It was a good call. If Chuck could get Lee down and start pounding his ribs or get him into a chokehold, this fight would be over in seconds.

But Lee ducked out of Chuck's hold fast as lightning, his elbow driving into Chuck's side on the way out with an audible snap. Chuck grunted, distracted. Lee had sickly sharp elbows. Unfortunately, I knew that from experience!

Lee landed a punch straight to the man's gut. Bent over, Chuck wasn't going down easily. He drove his head right into Lee's chest. Lee grunted as he staggered back, about to lose his balance. Somehow, he managed to get a hold of himself, swinging his foot up for a roundhouse kick. It clipped Chuck's shoulder, and from the way he cried out, I figured he already had an injury there.

They went on like this for a few more minutes, sweat pouring, grunting and growling, and the rest of us cheering overtop of the rising battle. Finally, Lee landed one more solid blow to that injured shoulder, and Chuck tapped out. "I've had enough," he gasped, rubbing his injuries and stepping back into the circle of testosterone-hyped men.

Lee shrugged and walked back into the appreciative crowd. It was a struggle to fight and not punch your opponent in the face. It took a ton of self-discipline, expending an incredible amount of energy. Sometimes we lost control and a blow or two would make it to the face. Horace was true to his word, and those who broke the rules or had bruised faces, had to take a break from the fighting until it healed up. If someone inflicted those injuries too many times, they were asked to leave the club altogether. It worried me, but I understood the logic. If we were caught, there was no telling what would happen.

Breaking the law wasn't something people *did* in New Colony. Not when doing so meant you'd disappear, sometimes your family right along with you. It was said by the royals that people out of line were simply relocated, given different assignments, a chance to be rehabilitated, but I had my doubts. I knew how my father was, knew the kind of loyalty he expected out of the people here, and he was only one cog in a wheel. What really happened to the ones who disappeared?

I shook off the worries and focused back on the room, wondering when I'd be healed enough to box again. I needed to get back in there. Even though I was one of the few young ones in the room, that didn't lessen my need to release my anger. Most of these men were older, but age didn't matter here. Fighting was our outlet, our way to make sense of the world. It was a risk to be here. A huge risk. But some risks weren't even a question. They were worth it. Some of us were here to learn how to defend ourselves. Some were here to feed the need. I was here for both.

I am not my father's son.

I was here to learn how to defend myself. At least, that's what I repeated in my head. At least, my own burning need to punch something had nothing to do with harming innocent people. I'd leave that sick desire to people like my father and Bryce. I had this intense wildness inside myself that I'd channeled into a single goal: one day getting back at my father for all the times he beat me as a child, and all the times he verbally and emotionally destroyed my mother. Every opponent I faced morphed into him. Time and time again, I fantasized what it would be like to fight back when he'd unleashed his anger on me. But even since he'd stopped physically harming me, it didn't change how I needed to be ready. It was only a matter of time before he lashed out again.

I watched the next three fights from the sideline, joking with the guys around me, enjoying myself as best as I could, imagining myself in the fighter's places. What moves would I make? How would it feel to be the one to land that kick? To receive that punch to the gut? But it did little to quench the fire. Actually, it did the opposite.

Stupid Bryce. This was his fault.

Of course he squeezed in next to me and shot me a smirk at that very moment. My jaw and fists clenched and I sucked in an frustrated breath.

"You hate that I'm the only other kid at school who

knows about this place, don't you?" He asked casually, ignoring the guys around him who looked at him the same way I did, like he was a leech.

"I certainly wouldn't have told you," I shot back. I hadn't told anyone, not even Tyler. It had been my glorious secret for nearly two years, and then a few months ago, Bryce showed up and ruined my sanctuary.

"I bet you've been wondering how I found Horace, huh? How did little ol' Bryce get an invitation to a place like this?"

I shrugged. I wanted to know, sure, but there was nothing I could do about it now. I caught Lee's eye from where he stood a few feet away. He was shaking his head, equally annoyed with Bryce's crap.

Bryce only grinned and laughed under his breath. "I'm not going to tell you, but only because I know how badly you want me to."

I rolled my eyes, thinking about my own journey to this place.

I'd found my way to this club when Horace had sat next to me on the Metro a few years ago. I'd noticed his cracked knuckles with their angry scabs. I'd assumed he was like my dad, and I don't know what came over me. I was only fourteen, but I laid into him. I told him what a complete and utter waste of skin he was, what a horrible human being he was for hurting other people.

Innocent people. How I hoped he got what was coming to him.

He'd stared at me for a long minute, but then ignored me and moved further down the train car. That had pissed me off, the anger burrowing so deep that it had leached me of all energy until the idiot was all I could think of. I wanted to smash his face in, wanted to make him pay. So a few days later when I saw him in the same Metro car, I'd purposely sat next to him. And the whole exchange started over again. But that time, Horace had shut me up, mentioning an address. He whispered to me that they met for an hour after work, that it was a secret club, and maybe I should stop by sometime. He added that it was the kind of secret that could get me killed if I wasn't careful, but I could learn how to fight whatever demons were living in my mind and home. He must've known. Must have seen my father in my vengeful eyes. Thank God he did, and that I found this place.

I turned on Bryce, looking him up and down. His prep-boy perfect hair and smirk weren't enough to make me hate him. That was common for our school. No, it was his entitled attitude. It was how much he reminded me of Dad. It was the way he goaded me on and pushed my buttons; the satisfaction he got from hurting other people just for the fun of it. I'd had enough of him for today.

I made my way toward the exit of the warehouse, pushing through the crowd of men. There were about forty of us now, all regulars, most coming nearly every day for at least an hour. I knew them all by name. Many felt like brothers to me. But I needed to get out of here before I messed up and broke Horace's rules. Not having a turn, knowing I'd have to wait a few more days to pummel into someone, killed me.

I found my jacket and bag in the pile by the door, about ready to push my way outside. My eyes scanned the group one last time, catching on a familiar set of shoulders. Shock rocketed through my body. I froze, staring with disbelief and horror. My father was here, just on the edge of the crowd, watching the fight. My heart exploded, pounding so loudly I heard the blood rushing through my ears. What was he doing here? Had he followed me? Had someone invited him to our club? But, we weren't allowed to invite others; this was Horace's thing. He did the inviting. And Horace was not the type of man my father would ever associate with. A deep sense of foreboding trickled down my spine. Something wasn't right.

Standing on the outskirts, he went unnoticed. He turned, no longer watching the fights. He was watching me. Our eyes connected in a clash of anger. Without a shadow of a doubt, I knew he'd come here for me. His face hardened, jaw tight with fury. He knew what I was capable of now. *Yeah, that's right, don't you dare try to fight me again. I'm stronger than you.*

But there was something else behind the fury in his eyes and his firm stance, something I didn't like seeing here. Smugness. What did he know that I didn't?

FOUR

I strode forward and stood in front of him, my arms crossed, standing tall as I stared him down. He was a mirror on the outside, looking so similar to me with our black hair and eyes, our creamy bronzed skin stretched over high cheekbones. His lip twitched up in a half smile.

"What are you doing here?" I asked in a low whisper.

The men around us were oblivious, focusing on the fight building to its peak. The noise of fists pummeling skin and men calling out allowed our conversation to stay hidden, at least for now. I hoped I could get him out of here before anyone realized he was an outsider. I didn't know how they'd react, but I didn't want to find out.

"I should be asking you the same thing," His

temper had faded to nonchalance. I knew better than to trust it. Me being here was a huge deal. But these fights were my chance, my training, my salvation, and my opportunity to take him down. And now that he knew it, he would hate me even more.

"Don't worry, Son." He grinned slowly, eyes looking me up and down. "There's still a chance for you to redeem yourself." He sniffed the air distastefully and glanced around. "Too bad I can't say the same for the rest of them." Then he sidestepped past me and strode purposefully around the edge of men and toward the exit.

I followed, shaking, fearful, and entirely unsure of what to expect. It couldn't be this easy. He wasn't just going to leave and be done with it. Something was wrong. He stopped at the door and I followed close at his heels, the light creeping around the edges into the dark room like a promise.

"I already worked out a deal for you, Tristan." Dad pressed a hand against the heavy door. "Once again, I had to clean up your mess."

Accusation burned at the back of my throat.

"What did you do?" I asked, my voice coming out hoarse.

But I already knew.

He stepped back from the rusted door just before it burst open. New Colony police flooded the room.

Their numbers were far too substantial for us to stand a chance. They descended on the crowd of men, swift as an ax, arresting them without question. I pressed myself against the far wall, outraged to see my friends being thrown to the ground. Shock woke me from a sort of trance when a handful of Royal Officers entered the warehouse. Dressed in pressed white uniforms, these men were the worst of the bad news. Anytime police showed up, things weren't good, but Royal Officers? My stomach twisted, guilt raking me from top to bottom. Royal Officers didn't just punish people, they made them disappear. My father talked to one of them, pointed to me, said something under his breath, then slinked off to the shadows.

"Nobody move," the very same officer yelled out, taking the lead. He wasn't the biggest man in the group, but his demeanor was the strongest—a born leader. The head to toe white uniform was standard for those officers who worked in the palace, directly with the royals. Whoever this man was, he wasn't someone to be trifled with. The room fell into silence, the realization sweeping through the crowd like a virus. Men blinked in disbelief, their complexions going pale, their eyes widening. Fear wasn't something I often saw in these men, and seeing it now nearly killed me.

"Everybody on the ground," the Royal Officer continued, "and put your hands behind your back."

There was no use in fighting, so none of us bothered. The officers had guns pointed. They had authority. We had nothing.

"I said get down," the officer grunted in my direction and I fell to my knees, my own fears beginning to
multiply.

Dad turned his back and strode toward the crowd
of police handcuffing our crew with zip ties, like he was
overseeing this entire operation. I knew he didn't have
the highest ranking title here, but seeing the way he
looked at my friends made me sick. We were under
arrest, but that was only the beginning of our problems.
If my father had anything to do with it, these men
wouldn't be given an ounce of leniency. Bile burned in
my throat and heat pricked at my eyes. This was my
fault.

My limbs felt like they were being filled with sand.
My head started to spin. The next thing I knew, my
cheek was flush against the cool cement, my face
pressed into the wall. Someone held my hands back
against my body, restraining them in a tight zip tie that
cut deeply into my wrists. "Don't move an inch," the
voice sneered before leaving me. And I waited. I
waited to be taken away. To be tried. To experience
whatever consequence was to be my punishment.

It could've been minutes, it could've been an hour,
but sometime later I was hauled to my feet. Father

stood off to one side, his mouth set in a grim line. He'd had me followed and been the one to alert the authorities, I was absolutely sure of that fact. There was no other explanation. Why would he do that? Did he really hate me so much that he'd want to get me arrested? It was a stupid question. Of course he did.

I shook out my legs, needles of pain prickling each one, and with several deep breaths, the fog finally cleared from my mind. Now that I could see the warehouse room again, my heart sank. The older men, my friends, they were all gone. Even our leader, Horace, was nowhere to be found. What would happen to them? Bryce was still in the room, restrained like me. But we were the last of us left. We were also the only ones under eighteen. When Horace had brought me in at age fourteen, I'd been the youngest by almost a decade. It stayed that way until Bryce had shown up a few months ago.

"Load these boys up," the Royal Officer who'd taken the lead said with a resigned tone. "These two are coming with us."

I walked, arms still restrained, and did my best to ignore the shoves from behind that caused me to stumble.

My father appeared at my side, his eyes a dangerous mix of light and dark. "Like I said, you have no idea how lucky you are to have me," he whispered low in my ear. "I took mercy on you. I preemptively did what I had to do to protect you. Don't you dare mess this up. I won't save you again."

"Lucky?" I replied, stuck on the word he'd used. I refused to look at his disgraceful face. "I'm the opposite of lucky to have you for a father. Nothing about this situation is protecting me."

He only sighed. "Like I said," he continued, "I made a deal for you. Don't screw it up."

He stomped off before I could utter a reply. He made a deal for me? What was that supposed to mean? I didn't know what to believe. If my father was involved, it couldn't be good. But then again, he was a powerful man. He worked for the kingdom and was one of the most important financial advisors in his department.

I was pushed out of the warehouse, the sunset casting everything in a monochromatic blinding light. A black van waited with the back open and Bryce and I were shoved inside. There were no comfy seats and we had to sit with our backs and cuffed hands pressed against hard metal walls. I tried to keep my breathing steady and my mind clear, but was falling prey to worried thoughts of what could be next for me.

"All right, you two." The lead Royal Officer stood with his hands on the back doors. He stared at us as if we were cockroaches he wanted to smash under his boot. We were a problem he was being forced to deal with, but he'd rather get rid of. Maybe we were. "I'm Royal Officer Hank Reynolds. And you are my newest recruits."

Before we could ask what he meant by that, he slammed the doors with a sharp thud, plunging us into darkness.

FIVE

"Get out," A gruff voice cut through the darkness as the van doors flew open, metal hinges creaking. Officer Reynolds stood waiting with that same grim expression he'd worn back at the warehouse. "You'll begin training here and if you're lucky enough to make the cut, then eventually, you could even end up at the palace. But I wouldn't count on it."

"What the hell are you talking about? What are we training for?" Bryce asked, jumping down to the gravel. I climbed out of the van, shaking out my legs and wondering the same thing. Night had fallen during our short drive and the humid air had turned sticky. One of Reynolds' men used scissors on our zip-ties, freeing our wrists. I stretched my arms forward with an audible crack of joints, but the relief was short-lived.

"Come on," Reynolds said, ignoring Bryce's question. He turned and strode purposefully toward the building. Gravel crunched under his leather boots, a street light illuminating his body. I pegged him for early forties. His dark cropped hair, bulging muscles, and cocky attitude showed his age.

He didn't stop to check if we followed.

Bryce shot me a scathing look and swaggered off after Reynolds. Did he think this was my fault? He was the idiot who'd punched me in the face. If it wasn't for him, my father wouldn't have had me followed in the first place. Because surely, that's what he'd done. I forced the questions and underlying guilt to the back of my mind and caught up with the others.

The building was one of the modern government buildings a few blocks north of the palace. Tall barbed wire fences surrounded the place with a few guards milling about. It reminded me of my dad's office in the financial sector, the building jutting into the inky sky, all polished chrome and tinted glass. Entering was what I imagined booking into a prison was like. It was stark white and smelled of chemical cleaners, but that was the least of my problems.

First up, Bryce and I were taken through a security search where a burly guy patted us down head to toe and then ushered us through a metal detector. A pile of folded clothes, light gray and plain, with a pair of shiny black boots sitting atop were shoved into our arms, and we were ushered into cubicles to change. I discarded my shorts, polo, and sneakers into a stainless steel bin in the corner and laced up my new boots. The whole time my mind was in two places: observing my surroundings, and dissecting what Officer Reynolds had said before.

He thought we might one day be at the palace.

That made little sense. I wasn't on track to be a Royal Officer. Granted, I hadn't taken my placement exams yet, but I had a thing for math, loved numbers, and was likely to be assigned a career in the same field as my father. Now, I suddenly found myself labeled as a new recruit. But for what? As far as I knew, Royal Officers were elite guards and police.

Bryce and I went back into what appeared to be the main hallway. I eyed Hank and his palace officer uniform. What did he actually *do* at the palace? That information wasn't public knowledge. They worked for the royal family—that was all I really knew. I couldn't imagine working with the royals. They always seemed so uptight, so elusive and unreachable.

After a couple left turns and a long walk down a brightly lit corridor, Reynolds led us into some kind of military barrack. Metal bunk beds lined one wall of the room with an opened bathroom door stationed to the left. Guys around my age strode about, seemingly enjoying some free time, if their casual chatting and laughter indicated anything. They were all dressed in the grayish uniforms Bryce and I now wore. The outfit felt like pajamas, stretchy and soft. I shook my head. This was so weird.

All at once, the guys seemed to notice Officer Reynolds standing in their doorway. They jumped up from whatever they were doing, some playing cards, a few reading, most chatting, and stood at attention. Once again, I wondered why this Royal Officer was so damn important.

"You've got two new friends," Reynolds said gruffly. "Make them feel welcome." Then in a flash, he turned on his heel and was gone, closing the door behind him, a lock clicking into place. Bryce and I exchanged a worried glance and I let out a breath. This was definitely not what I had expected to happen when I'd left for school this morning

Silence settled over the room as the group of twenty or so guys studied us. A few glared, some rolled their eyes, others looked away. Collectively, they didn't seem all that impressed. Bryce rolled his shoulders and cracked his knuckles like his idiot self, and I certainly didn't blame these guys for thinking we were a couple of tools.

"What happened to him?" A mousy-looking dude snickered, pointing to my face. I'd forgotten all about the bruises and automatically reached out to touch my sore cheek.

"I beat him up," Bryce said with a smug smile, and then strode over to the one empty bunk. He laid himself on the bottom and put his arms behind his ugly head, like he owned the place. Prick.

Guess that means I get the top bunk. I didn't move in that direction, but instead I scanned the group, seeking out the guy I'd pegged as the alpha. He looked hard, like a lot of the men I'd boxed with. He stood with ropy arms crossed over a broad chest, his muscles flexing naturally. A few of the others kept glancing his way, waiting to see what would happen next.

"I'm Tristan." I reached out my hand. He stared at it warily but after a long second shook it. His grip was iron tight.

"Jose," he replied, dark eyes softening slightly as he released his hand and folded his arms again.

"Mind telling me what this place is, Jose?"

Everyone had turned to faced us by now, eager to get a peek at the new guy, I guess. But judging from their snickers, *that* was not the question they'd expected out of me

"You mean you don't know?" Jose smiled for real this time, and it lit up his face like a beacon. Maybe he'd gained his leadership role not from intimidation, but because he was a likable kid with a knack for bringing people together. I hoped that was the case. "Nah, it's okay," he said. "They don't always tell. I forget that some of the guys didn't apply for this."

"Apply for what?" I tried to sound friendly, but it came out hard and I immediately regretted it.

Jose cronies stiffened but he wasn't bothered. "You, Tristan, are officially a Royal Officer in training." He lifted his eyebrows, anticipating my reaction.

I took a step back even though I had pretty much worked this out by now. The confirmation still stung. A Royal Officer? Me?

It didn't make sense. Bryce and I had been breaking the law. All those other men, many I considered my friends and mentors, had undoubtedly been arrested. So, what, the two who happened to be teenagers got a free pass? But I remembered my father's comments about how lucky I was to have him. How he'd made a deal for me. I let out a deep breath and rubbed my hands across my face, everything clicking into place. Dad had pulled strings all right, somehow managing to land me here instead of a jail cell. But this was never the plan for me.

"What kind of job does a Royal Officer do?" I pressed. They were an elusive group, one that held high authority, but it wasn't like I'd ever been to the palace to see them in action.

Bryce sauntered over to stand next to me, his

earlier smugness now gone. His presence bugged me and I shifted away, ignoring the urge to elbow him in the rib cage. I didn't want to be associated with him.

"Yeah," Bryce said sharply, trying to sound intimidating. "What does that even mean?" *Trying* being the key word: he sounded like the whiney prep-school kid he was. At least we weren't in those ridiculous school uniforms anymore.

"Royal Officers," Jose said and raised an eyebrow, stepping closer to me, "police magic."

I studied him, wanting this all to be an elaborate joke, some kind of lesson. But one look in Jose's eyes and I knew it was true. Bryce and I had inadvertently landed in dangerous territory, and I didn't know how to feel about that. The Royal Officers were highly ranked, and it seemed they were more than just glorified police offers. Their program was one of the most competitive to get into out of all of the officer training programs, but I never realized magic was involved.

"That's right," Jose said with an amused lilt to his voice. "We're the ones who make sure the Guardians of Color stay in line. Can't let them use their alchemy for evil."

I'd heard of the color magic before. Everyone had. That alchemy existed was common knowledge, but it was rare, and I'd never seen it in action. Nor did I have a clue what it *actually* was. A tingle of anticipation ran down my spine at the prospect of working so closely with something so mysterious.

"You'd better watch your back, new kids," Jose continued, "Those alchemists, they're more powerful than you can even imagine."

SIX

My knuckles cracked against the hard leather, the punching bag swinging with each *thud, thud, thud* of my beating fists. Sweat dripped down my forehead, and the air-conditioned breeze swept over the back of my neck. I zeroed in on the target and focused all my pent-up anger into each blow. I pictured my father's gloating face.

Harder.

Wondered what had happened to Horace and the guys at the warehouse, my brothers.

Faster.

Felt the silence of my timid mother, home alone and worried.

A feral scream escaped my mouth. I attacked the bag, all the building frustration let loose in a torrent of rage.

Pound! Pound! Pound!

"Oh man, what did that thing ever do to you?" Someone snickered, bringing me out of my focus. I turned toward TJ, one of the guys who typically hung out with Jose.

"Hey, don't be jealous." I grinned. That one small muscle movement somehow relaxed me. Geez, maybe I was a little too intense lately.

"I'm just glad I'm not on your bad side." TJ rolled his eyes. "You're an animal." He bounded over to practice on the bag next to mine. It only took a couple of his thwacking punches for me to realize what I must look like compared to the other guys. Illegal or not, the years in the warehouse had paid off. I forced a cocky grin down. I didn't know if I even wanted to be a Royal Officer, but I knew I didn't want to be a snob.

"Tristan." A deep voice boomed from across the gym. "Get over here."

Reynolds.

I forced my nerves settle down as I jogged across the room, pretending not to notice the twenty pairs of eyeballs that followed me.

For the last month all of us recruits been training day in and out. Everybody was getting stronger and faster. Our trainers were pretty tight-lipped, but they sure knew how to fight and wield a weapon. Other than the physically grueling workouts, weapons training, and meals, we hadn't done much else. We hadn't even left the training base. No contact with the outside world. No letters from home. Nothing.

"Yes, Sir." I stood in front of Officer Reynolds, still breathing hard from the workout. I ran my sweaty hands down the black nondescript athletic gear and tried to focus.

"Walk with me." He turned on his heel and took off. I followed him out of the gym and began the long descent through the modern hallway. From being extra observant and asking lots of questions since my arrival, I'd figured out that the building was specifically for training potential officers, whatever their field may be. They'd bring new recruits in here in waves; each of the trainings taking a couple months to complete. If we made it out of here, it would hopefully be to the palace next. If we didn't, I had no idea what would happen to me.

"How long have you been fighting?" Reynolds asked.

"I dunno, I guess we've been here about a month." I shrugged.

He shook his head. "You know what I mean. The warehouse I picked you up from—how long have you been going there to fight?"

"A few years," I answered through gritted teeth.

"You have talent," he continued. "I don't know if I've ever seen anyone who can punch the stuffing out of bag like you can. Honestly, I'm impressed."

I shrugged, pushing down a mix of pride and rage. I wanted to yell at him, tell him how much Horace had helped me, how all those guys were innocent of anything besides breaking a law that shouldn't be there in the first place, but I held it in. "Thanks," I said instead.

We walked into a shiny and barren office, a single desk and a few metal folding chairs strewn about.

"Ignore the mess," he said. "It's only temporary. We'll be out of here soon."

I tried not to get excited about that because, truth be told, I was starting to hate this place. Getting out could mean getting to finally see magic, and even better, maybe I'd get to see Mom again.

"Most of these kids aren't going to make it to the palace," he said casually as we sat down. "They won't ever become Royal Officers. We only take the best and brightest. Sure, some of them may work in law enforcement, but not with me."

"Okay?" The question stretched out in confusion.

"I think you have what it takes," he continued. "Your father told me to keep an eye on you and he was right. You may be just what I'm looking for."

I clenched my hands into fists and looked away. My father was behind this. He had been talking to Reynolds, and nothing about that sat well with me. "Thank you, Sir."

"But I also have my suspicions."

I turned back and scrutinized what I saw. Middle aged, with dark salt-and-peppered hair, fit as any guy in this building, intelligence gleaming behind intense eyes, and every bit as uptight.

"Suspicions?"

"I'm sure it's no surprise that you're only here because your father is an old friend of mine. I owed him a favor. *You* are that favor."

Heat rose in my belly. "And what about Bryce?"

He sighed. "Bryce caught a lucky break and was in the right place at the right time. We'll see if he can keep it."

Right place, right time? I fought the urge to roll my eyes. I didn't want to be here if it meant my friends from the boxing club weren't with me, but I also didn't want to be rotting in a prison cell either. And as much as I missed my mom, wanted to be there for her, it had been nice these last few weeks away from my father. At least there was an upside to this.

"I suspect," Reynolds continued, "that you don't want to be a Royal Officer. Am I correct in ascertaining that you're only going through the motions here?"

I held his gaze, caught off by his astute observation. Was I that easy to read? He stared back and I caught something trustworthy gleaming in his eyes. I let out a breath and considered how to say this the right way.

"I don't know yet," I said honestly. "I never thought I'd be an officer, but I like to train, to fight, and I wouldn't mind a job where I got to protect innocent people from bad guys. Whoever they are—"

I thought of my dad.

"If you join us," Reynolds said, smiling, "you'll get to do those things."

"But I don't like being away from my mother."

Reynolds smile quirked, teasing. "Are you home-sick? I didn't peg you for a mama's boy."

"Proud of it." I laughed, my hard exterior finally cracking even as my heart dropped. I did miss her, but more than that, I felt immense guilt.

I wanted to tell him everything on my mind. I wanted to trust him. What would he do if he knew his old friend, my father, was a monster who beat his son and controlled his wife? My temper was a dying ember compared to his flame. I itched to speak it, to say it all, but something held me back. Could I really trust him? I barely knew him. And anyway, he probably wouldn't believe me.

"Well, you're here for now." He sighed and leaned

back in his chair. "I'd like to see what you're capable of. If I'm right, you'll make a great addition to my team. But I brought you in here to tell you something important."

"And what's that?"

"I don't take reluctant soldiers. I work with the loyal, the proud, and the ones who are willing to put everything else aside for a greater cause."

And I was reluctant, wasn't I? I wanted to be home with Mom, but I didn't know how to protect her, or if she even wanted it. My father had the power. I'd broken the law every time I'd gone to that warehouse. If I took my father on, I likely wouldn't end up back home, but in a jail cell instead. At least this way, I would get to train. Maybe make something of myself. Maybe one day I could take him down. Maybe this was where I needed to be, at least for right now. I swallowed hard, making a decision.

"I want to be here," I said firmly. "I want to see where this goes. I think this may be the best thing for me now."

Reynolds eyed me, a slow smile spreading across his tanned face, his teeth gleaming white. "Attaboy."

"So what's next?"

"All this training, it's only phase one. I'll be letting at least half of the guys go soon. You won't be joining them. It'll be on to phase two for you, where you'll really be tested."

I raised an eyebrow. "How so?"

"That's for me to know and you to find out."

SEVEN

"Watch where you're going." Bryce slammed his bony shoulder into mine, pushing past me into the shared bathroom. I stilled, forcing myself not to jump the guy. Reynolds wasn't kidding about the group being culled before phase two. Over half the group was reassigned to other officer trainings, and a few weaklings even got sent home. Unfortunately, Bryce was one of the nine who still remained.

I glared and tried to ignore the sickening crunch of Bryce popping his neck as I headed into the bathroom to brush my teeth. He was only here because he was a nasty fighter. Reynolds said Royal Officers had to be skilled at combat, and those of us left were all the same: angry guys who liked to hit things and had something to prove. As much as I hated Bryce, even I had to admit we had that in common. We'd stayed out of each other's way, but now with so few of us left, that was getting harder and harder to do.

He pressed his knuckles together, cracking them all at once, while he stared at himself in the mirror trying to look hard. He had a thing for popping his joints, and every time I heard the cracking sound, my stomach roiled. Yet, this morning, it wasn't just Bryce who had my nerves elevated. Actually, the same nervous energy was so strong with all nine of us, it was practically visible.

Today was the day we'd been waiting for.

Today we were meeting the color alchemists.

Once the group had dwindled down to nine, we'd been educated on the details of color alchemy. We didn't know all there was to know quite yet, but we knew why color magic was valuable and dangerous. Basically, every alchemist was different. Some could use certain colors and not others. And every color had a different ability or magic attached to it. Reynolds had said that yellow, for example, could make an alchemist faster and stronger than the average human. Green? That could be used for healing.

I splashed icy water on my face, letting it buoy up my excitement, then shut off the faucet and gave myself a quick stare down. I was looking forward to seeing magic in action, and the nerves needed to go.

"You ready for this, man?" TJ asked, as I sauntered

back to my bunk to change into the white outfit we'd been assigned to wear for the day. Apparently they wanted us to blend in with the other Royal Officers.

"Ready as I'll ever be." I shrugged, and then shoved my arm into the sleeve.

TJ scratched at his curly black hair. "When they say they're dangerous, how dangerous do you think they mean?"

I didn't have an answer for him.

"Very dangerous." Jose stepped into the conversation, something he did quite often. He was a natural born leader, the kind of guy who made friends easily. So no one was surprised to see him still heading up the group. Still here, and with nobody wanting to take the leadership role away from him—myself included. The way I saw it, Jose was nice enough, smart as a whip, and had never caused any trouble for me.

"How would you know if they're dangerous?" TJ asked, his voice low, a green eye twitching, probably from stress.

Jose glanced from side to side, but it was just the three of us hanging around my bunk. "I don't know if I should tell you this..." He smiled softly, lost in thought. "Okay, truth is, I grew up next door to an alchemist. Her parents kept it secret long as they could, but eventually she accidentally exposed her secret. She left when we were nine. I never forgot what she could do though."

"No way." TJ's jaw fell open and his twitchy eye narrowed. "Did you ever see her do her magic?"

Something inside me perked at that, intrigued. To actually see magic? But, the craziest thing, we'd probably be seeing it within the hour.

"Well." Jose's smile faltered. "As a matter of fact, I did see it. Like I said, we were friends. I knew about her secret for years before she got caught, so yeah, you could say I've seen the magic."

"No kidding." TJ shook his head, clearly more in awe of his leader than ever. "She never freaked you out or anything?"

"No," Jose replied, his voice clipped. But then he sighed and shook his head. "Not at all. Though she probably should have."

He dug the tip of his shoe into the floor. I wondered about him for a second, wondering what kind of secrets he was hiding. We all had a secret or two, right? But I couldn't figure this guy out. Jose was one who'd applied to this training, and from the way he trained, he clearly wanted to be here more than anybody. Maybe the experience with his friend had helped him see something about alchemy that I didn't see. As much as it intrigued me, the thought of magic freaked me out a little. It was a foreign concept and miles beyond normal human limitation. But like I'd told Reynolds, I wanted to see where this whole recruitment process could take me.

The door swung open and Reynolds appeared with four of his men, all dressed in white Royal Officer uniforms. Today I would be wearing the same thing, just without any of the decorative emblems. I had to admit, getting out of these gray cottons would be nice.

"All right, you nine are the remaining men out of what was quite honestly a group full of pathetic boys. Congratulations."

We couldn't help it, we clapped. Bryce let out a deep whoop, and I rolled my eyes.

"That's the good news," Reynolds said, pacing in front of us. "The bad news is, only five of you will become Royal Officers."

We fell silent, the air practically sucked from the room.

"Five of you men here and five women from the female training class will have that honor."

So only ten new recruits each year? It didn't seem like a lot, but then I didn't know what went on at the palace.

Reynolds stopped pacing and studied us, his head cocked in contemplation. "And even then, we don't expect all ten of the new recruits to last more than a year or two." He frowned. "Quite frankly, not everyone is cut out to work with alchemists. They're powerful. Our job is to keep them in line. But they're also human. They look, think, and feel like you and me. And if you allow yourself to become too close, too compassionate with them, then you shouldn't expect to keep your job."

My eyes flicked to Jose, remembering the way he'd spoken of his old friend. He glared at Reynolds, the first time I'd ever seen him look angry. Oh yeah, there was something going on with him. Interesting.

"So we're essentially their babysitters?" TJ asked with a chuckle. "Are they hot? Because if so, then I'm cool with that."

"Watch your mouth," Reynolds replied with a jolt. "Royal Officers aren't babysitters. We're the enforcers. And you shouldn't look at alchemists that way. Not ever. Now, let's go." He turned toward the door. "It's about time you met a few of them."

We followed and he added one last thought. "Be on your guard because color isn't the only thing they're known to manipulate."

EIGHT

Even with the level of importance my father carried, my family had never been invited to the palace. I was sure that bothered him to no end. The royals were known for their parties, but an invitation had never graced our doorway. I went to school with those kinds of families, and we were almost that kind of family, but not quite. So to be walking the halls of the palace felt pretty surreal. I ignored the battle of warring emotions fighting it out inside my body and focused on the tour. I shouldn't care about this place. I shouldn't be excited. I was not my social-climbing father. And yet, chills ran over my entire body.

"If you make it with us," Reynolds said, "then you'll live here when you're not out on some kind of mission for the King."

"You all live here?" TJ asked, shaking his head. "I

mean, it's pretty cool, but don't you have a wife or something?"

The group chuckled. Once again, TJ had opened his mouth and said what we'd all been thinking. We were teenage boys, Bryce and I being the youngest of the pack, and I for one didn't want to grow up to be some kind of palace eunuch.

"Some officers live off campus with their families and rotate in," Reynolds said gruffly, "but that's rare. Most of us are married to our job."

Sounds hot...

We continued down the ornate hallway, one I'd seen in photographs and newscasts countless times. It was a mix of old and new, some of the guilded walls and artifacts from the time before, when America was still intact and the people living here were elected, and the rest was comprised of modern sleek glass and polished floors.

"It's easier if the Royal Officers live here, since we work right alongside the alchemists, and they live here."

"And about half the officers are female, right?" TJ laughed, good-boy dimples framing his wide mouth. His green eyes sparked with ballsy confidence. Reynolds surprised us all and laughed along.

"That is true," he said, with a quick raise of an eyebrow.

The palace had left the last of its colonial design behind, transforming completely to the modern glass and chrome of the added on wings, the same style as the training building we'd been living in, the same style of most official buildings. I relaxed. This felt more like home. Then I bristled at the thought. Did I really want this to be my home?

"You're in the Guardian's territory now."

I looked around, waiting to see one of them. Guardians of Color were their official title, but I'd always thought of them as alchemists.

We stepped through a regular doorway and into a gym that was three times the size of the one I'd been training in for the past month. Equipment I used every day—cross trainers, weights, bikes—surrounded a square matted area in the center. Officers stood to attention, stationed throughout the room, and some others worked out. In contrast to the stark white of their uniforms, the other people in the room wore black —the alchemists. And my eyes were immediately drawn to the center of the room, my breath taken, my heart beating out an irregular rhythm. A fight took place, grunts and groans I had become accustomed to hearing at the warehouse, but that's where the similarities ended. They fought in a way I could barely comprehend. Their strength was used to toss a person across the room or to pound them into the floor with a single blow.

"This is insane," TJ mumbled.

This was magic? We couldn't compete with this.

"Yellow alchemy, like I said," Reynolds announced calmly. "Come on, this isn't actually where we're supposed to be today. I just wanted you to take a look as to why it's so important you keep training in the gym."

A few of the alchemists had stopped their workout to watch us, their eyes either inquisitive or downright hostile. I joined my classmates and quickly found the exit. As much as I enjoyed a good fight, taking on one of those guys using yellow magic hardly seemed fair. I shook it off, forcing the thought to the back of my mind.

"And that's why the alchemists don't get to carry guns," TJ snickered, nodding toward Reynolds' gun strapped to a holster on his side.

"It makes sense, right, man?" TJ nudged Jose.

Jose shook his head slightly and looked back at the gym, his eyes darting around to take quick stock of the inhabitants. I couldn't help but wonder if he was looking for the girl he used to know. He was a savvy guy, smart, but he was being a little bit too obvious.

I elbowed him and caught his eyes, widening mine. "Careful," was all I said, but he paled and nodded.

We walked further down the hallway, past class

rooms with entire windowed walls, where magical lessons took place. Most were filled with teenagers or younger. I clenched my fists when I saw the youngest of the bunch, kids who couldn't be older than six. Alarm bells buzzed through my head. The little kids made me the most nervous. Should they be here? They were so tiny! Where were their parents? I swallowed hard, guessing that their parents had been removed from the equation. According to the royal family, it was never too early for alchemists to start learning their magic.

I'd been caught so off guard by the children that I'd fallen to the back of the group. We turned another corner, and something caught my attention. Was that crying? Yes, definitely the choking sobs of a child in distress. The crying wasn't the usual sound one would expect out of a kid. Something was different about it, wrong. Broken. In a split-second, I peeled off from the back of group to find the source. If it really was a child, and something bad was happening here, I needed to know about it before I agreed to become a Royal Officer.

I tiptoed along the edge of the wall, closer to the crying, steeling myself for a possible fight. Cautiously, I opened the closest door, and found a young girl, probably only ten or eleven years old. She sat in a mess of tears on the floor. The room was small, dark, and filled with purple. Purple rocks, furniture. Everything.

"You okay, kid?" I whispered, slipping into the room.

Her eyes shot up, ocean blue and shining with salty tears. "Who are you?"

"Tristan," I said, kneeling before her so I could assess her condition. She looked okay; no blood or anything.

"What are you doing here?" Her brow furrowed.

I smiled and relaxed my body. "Going on a tour, I guess. I heard you crying. Had to check it out."

She looked away and wiped the remaining tears. "Are you an alchemist? I don't think I've ever seen you before."

"No, definitely not an alchemist. I guess they want me to become a Royal Officer, maybe. I'm not sure if I want to do it."

"Trust me, you don't want to do it," she scoffed, her eyes hardening.

"Why do you say that?"

"This place, it's not what they say it is," she said, drawing out each word like a punch. "It's not good. We don't do good things here, we're bad."

Okay, that was creepy. I raised an eyebrow. "Bad? How so?"

She wrapped long arms around skinny knees "I

can't talk about it. It's ..." she paused, twisting her lips. "Private."

"Huh." I shrugged, but inside my senses were raised to high alert. "I guess that's understandable. Thanks for the heads-up." I let out a breath. I needed to ask. "You're sure you're okay? Nobody is hurting you, are they?"

She stood abruptly and laughed. "Trust me, Tristan," she said. "Nobody's hurting me. Unfortunately, it's the other way around." She gave me a sad smile and stormed from the room, her knobby knees shaking, her blonde hair flashing in the morning light of the hallway.

What had I just stumbled upon? The girl was pretty young to be saying such grown-up things. And she had been crying over what—the fact that she'd hurt somebody? I didn't understand, and I wasn't sure if I wanted to. I got up to leave, hoping I could catch up to my group quickly before my absence was noted and landed myself into major trouble.

"You have a big heart," a soft voice echoed from nowhere, and I nearly jumped out of my skin. Another girl, probably a few years older than me, emerged from the shadows. Geez, had she been there the whole time? I hadn't even seen her. She wore a flowy black gown with thin ropes of purple crystals layered around her neck.

"Who are you?" I asked, backing toward the exit.

"I should be asking you the same thing," she said. "I'm Lily. I'm known as the purple alchemist." She laughed, a crackling, unnatural sound, that made the tiny hairs on the back of my neck stand on end.

"Okay, so what's purple alchemy?" I asked, trying to act like she didn't worry me in the slightest. Total crap, of course. She was ten-times creepier than the other girl had been.

Lily grinned softly and stepped closer. Her eyes were so light blue they barely had any pigment, and her hair so blonde it was practically white. And there was something about her that didn't feel right; she seemed so tired. Purple bruises darkened the bags under her eyes, and the energy I got from her was pure exhaustion beyond reason.

"Purple is quite special," she said, tilting her head inquisitively. "Why don't I just show you?"

I gulped, reaching for the door handle. I needed to get out of here. But my feet had a mind of their own, because they kept me rooted in place. Lily touched a stone that hung from one of the cords around her neck. Purple filtered out of it and into the air, swirling around us in magical tendrils. Then, much to my disbelief, it trickled into the two of us, somehow connecting us. I felt it immediately, like an energetic rope tying me to Lily. I blinked, unable to utter a word.

My hands shook, my heart sped. A bead of sweat dripped down the side of my neck. The magic between us swelled.

"Is this alchemy?" I finally gasped.

Yes, she said, but her mouth didn't move. I was staring right at her when she said it, so I would have noticed.

Are you reading my mind? I asked the question in my mind, feeling like an idiot for believing this could be real.

Yes, she said again. *At least, what you want to tell me, I can hear.* And again, she spoke this right into my head, her mouth never moving.

Amazing.

She began speaking, ready to have a conversation entirely in our thoughts. *Purple alchemy is used for telepathy, like right now, as well as reading the future. Though, I don't always have control over when that's going to happen. Everyone wants their future read. The King, especially. I haven't quite got a handle on that one yet. He's been working me into the ground to try to figure it out.*

Her face fell, the tiredness returning to her features.

You know the King?

The door pushed open, hitting me in the back. I stepped forward just as an angry voice filled the small space. "What are you doing in here?" Reynolds demanded.

Dread spread wide as I turned to him. I held up my hands, my heart thudding in my chest. "I'm so sorry," I said. "I heard a little girl crying and came to check on her. I thought ... I dunno what I thought. But, she's fine. She left just now, but then I met this woman, Lily." I was rambling and we both knew it.

Reynolds shook his head at Lily, pointing at her. "You know better, Lily. What were you thinking?"

Then he grabbed my arm and pulled me from the room. "Stick with the tour, Tristan," he snapped, hissing under his breath so only I could hear, "I can't overlook something like that again. If you know what's good for you, you won't show compassion toward the alchemists."

"I'm sorry," I muttered, my cheeks flaming and my fists tight at my sides. Since when was compassion a crime?

He let out a breath, continuing in a hushed whisper. "Listen, Kid, my superior is newly promoted and on a mission to prove herself. She'll eat you alive if she finds you doing something like that."

I nodded, grateful and surprised he was revealing a kinder side of his personality for my sake. I glanced back toward the purple room. Lily still stood there, staring at me through the space in the open door. The light silhouetted her pale face in the darkness like a dying ember.

You don't have what it takes to be an officer, she said into my mind, *but you must make it through this phase, Tristan, you must. Your destiny depends on it. As does hers.*

Hers? Who are you talking about?

I don't see much, but I see that. I see you saving her, she said. Then she closed the door and we lost telepathic connection before I could ask anything more.

NINE

"And then there were seven." Reynolds shook his head and paced the length of the classroom. He did that a lot, the pacing thing. But I didn't think it made his job any easier.

The nine of us left had spent the last two weeks studying the ins and outs of alchemy. We knew all the different applications and the rules associated with color. Plus, with three visits to witness the alchemists in action at the palace, all of us should've been able to ace the exam.

Apparently not.

"As you know," Reynolds continued, "we needed you to pass this test to make it to the next phase. Two of you haven't managed that and will be reassigned to other officer trainings. Rest assured, you wouldn't have made it this far if you didn't have talent. You will still be able to have a fine career, but just not at the palace with the Guardians of Color."

A collective groan rung out, and we glanced at one another. Who would it be? Inwardly, I begged for Bryce's name to be announced. Nerves crept up my spine at the thought of getting kicked out of the program. I still wasn't convinced I wanted to be a Royal Officer, but Lily's words pestered me like a constant ringing in my ears.

You must make it through this phase, Tristan, you must. Your destiny depends on it.

What would happen if I failed her, whoever "she" was? I hated that Lily had somehow read my future and tied my destiny to a person without explaining who that person was. Could it be my mom? Someone else? Who was "she"? These questions had bothered me for weeks, and once again I shook the memory of Lily's voice from my mind to focus back on Reynolds.

"Kevin Greene and TJ Malone," he sighed, his face grim. "I'm sorry, boys, but it's the end of the road."

Kevin slammed his fist onto the desk. "Please, let me take the test again."

I didn't know the guy too well. He'd kept to himself, much like I had. But I could tell that he wanted to be here like he wanted air to breathe.

"I'm sorry." Reynolds said smoothly. "These aren't my rules. There's nothing I can do. Go now, and we'll be able to get you training for something equally as good."

"Yeah, right," he grumbled, then stalked out of the classroom in a rush of anger. I didn't blame him, honestly. Most of these guys would've been just as defensive as Kevin.

TJ wasn't as quick to leave, however. He'd made close friends with everyone, even Bryce. He was like-able and great comic relief for this intense process. TJ was always cracking the best jokes and was not both-ered by other people's faults, no matter how annoying they were. I sighed; I was going to miss him.

"Thank you for the opportunity," he said, shaking Reynolds' hand first. Then he went around to the rest of us and said his goodbyes, rueful chuckles and regretful mutters along the way. When he made it to me, I stood and took his hand with as much respect as I could muster.

"Take care of yourself," I said, wishing I had some-thing better to say.

"I always do." TJ smiled weakly, but it didn't quite reach his normally happy-go-lucky green eyes. I wondered what he meant by that, if he had a family back home he could rely on, or if he was more like me than I'd originally thought. I should have gotten to know him better, should have asked him about his life more, taken more of an interest. Now it was too late and all I was left with was guilt and another friend lost.

"Oh, it's okay," he said. "I've never been that great at test taking. I get nervous and forget everything I study. Truth is, I kind of saw this coming."

I dropped my head. "I'm sorry, man, that's not fair."

He shrugged. "Life's not fair, I guess."

He turned to leave, exiting the room with a quick wave and a playful wink. A few of Reynolds' men followed him out, and the room once again became lost in silence as we took our seats. I glanced around at those of us left, finding Bryce staring back at me with a sour look on his face.

"We're going on a trip," Reynolds' gravelly voice shook us from our thoughts. "Alchemists live and train in the palace, that's true. But they must travel around the kingdom often. There are several outposts where most of them end up staying for periods of time, so it should come as no surprise that Royal Officers must do the same. We'll be joining a group in the north. Once there, you'll have more contact with the alchemists and the officers than ever before."

"Nice," Bryce said with a smirk. "I'm ready to show those freaks who's boss."

I glared at him, wondering how he'd gotten this far. He wasn't that smart, or that great of a fighter beyond his recklessness, and he was as self-serving as they came. I looked to Reynolds, saw the way he gritted his teeth—I wasn't alone in my thinking. I smiled. Bryce would knock himself out of the running before long. All I needed to do was keep out of his way and wait for him to do it to himself.

"As I was saying." Reynolds narrowed his eyes at Bryce. "We will be joining a group out there, and you'll be expected to employ all of your training and to act as if you are already a Royal Officer. Part of that means showing respect for the alchemists and what they do."

Bryce shrunk in his seat, and Jose snickered.

"At the end of our trip,"—Reynolds looked over each of us—"the five of you who display the most aptitude for the job will be moved into the palace, and your new life will begin."

And the remaining two would be forgotten.

THE BUS CARRIED ALL of us, plus Reynolds' men, toward our final phase of training. Six hours in confined quarters with a bunch of sweaty, intense men and I was ready to crawl into a hole and never see another living being. My forehead rested against the cool window as I watched the forest fly by through bleary eyes. What had been miles and miles of the same green was changing into something I couldn't explain. I sat forward, squinting into the wilderness with disbelief.

"What is this place?" I asked under my breath. I shifted in my seat, hoping to find someone with an answer. The other recruits were just as fidgety.

The land on one side of the road was charred, almost like a fire had claimed every bit. Except this was different: there was no ash, no burned up bits or bare branches. It was simply ... gray.

"Settle down," Reynolds said from up front. He turned in his seat. "These are the Shadow Lands."

"But what are they?" Jose asked the obvious.

"You'll see soon enough," Reynolds replied, his voice carrying over the group. "It would do you lot some good to learn a bit of patience."

I scooted to the edge of my seat to where one of Reynolds' Royal Officers was slowly waking from sleep across the aisle. This guy wasn't as hardened as the others, so I hoped he didn't tear my head off for what I was about to do.

"Hey." I poked him in the shoulder. He didn't stir so I poked him again. "Hey, what is it with this place? Why is it all gray?" I whispered.

He blinked a few times, sat up alert, then looked around and sunk back into his seat. "Ah, it's just the Shadow Lands. It's nothing to worry about."

"But what happened here?" I asked, voice low. I wasn't giving up so easily.

"Relax, kid."

The bus turned abruptly, and I nearly lost my balance. I looked back at the officer, but he'd already shifted away from me and closed his eyes again. *Thanks anyway, pal.*

We slowed to a crawling pace before stopping in front of yet another modern government building with Royal Officers in white and color alchemists in black milling about. We shuffled off the bus, me being the last one. The humidity wasn't nearly as strong here as it was in the capital city. I took in a deep breath of the thin afternoon air and stretched out the cramps in my long legs.

"Inside you will find private living quarters and your very own Royal Officer uniform. Hurray," Reynolds said sarcastically, his eyes twinkling for the briefest of moments.

"What about a gun?" Bryce asked. For once Bryce's questions didn't drive me nuts. With all these unknowns wandering about, I wanted a gun to protect myself too.

"You won't get a gun until you've proved yourself responsible with one." Reynolds sighed. "Let's get going, we have things to do."

We followed him inside the bustling building, the

chrome and glass surfaces nearly identical to that of our previous housing, except this place was busy with officers and alchemists marching to unknown places. After being ushered to our individual rooms, we dressed and met in a common room, waiting for further instructions.

"What do you think that was back there?" Jose asked, leaning against the wall beside me.

"What? The Shadow Lands?"

He nodded.

"I don't know." I sighed.

"It kind of creeped me out."

"Me too, everything looked so wrong—off somehow."

"Dead," he supplied the word I'd been avoiding. "Everything looked dead."

An icy shudder ran down my body. Maybe Jose was right, maybe it was dead land. But dead didn't even seem to cover it. It had been worse than that, as if it wasn't only dead, but a shadow of what it had once been.

"Shadow Lands," I said, turning the phrase over in my head. Fitting. But now the real question wasn't *what* it was. I wanted to know what had done that. By whom? And most importantly, why?

"Gentlemen." Reynolds entered the room and we jumped up to stand at attention. He was blocking someone behind him in the doorway and a sense of importance ran through my body. He looked us up and down in our newly minted uniforms, a satisfied smile creeping to his face. "There's someone I'd like you to meet."

Then he pushed the door fully open, and from around the corner, someone strode into our common room with all the confidence in the world. A collective gasp echoed through the group. His Royal Majesty, King Richard Heart, stood before us, eyes of brilliant gray sweeping over the group like we were his shiny new toy. Maybe we were.

TEN

I stood frozen, my eyes bugging out of my head, almost unable to believe this moment was real and that I wasn't dreaming back on that godforsaken bus. I'd never thought I'd meet the King, and I especially never imagined it would happen under these circumstances. *This was crazy! How in the world did I end up all the way here?* My parents would faint with happiness if they could see me now. I wished I could tell Mom about this. Dad could die for all I cared. As far as I was concerned, he'd condemned all my friends back at the boxing club to death, if not something close to it. I'd never forgive him; it didn't matter that I was in the presence of royalty because of his choices over my future.

"Hello, young recruits," King Richard said, his voice smooth as silk. He was middle-aged with a presence that radiated power and charisma—a jarring combination, but immediately I felt it, his ability to command a room. He was all charisma on the news feeds but that didn't even compare to the real thing. "I'm glad you've made it this far," he said. "I asked your trainer to bring you here because I'm looking for something very specific in our upcoming class."

He said "specific" like someone would say "checkmate", as if he'd already won just by getting us out here. He paused and looked over the seven of us as if searching for the weakest link ... or maybe the strongest. The room prickled with nervous energy. His eyes landed on mine, and I held my breath, refusing to look away. I could do this. I could be what he needed, and if I wasn't? That was his loss.

"Well then." He smiled and looked away. "I think it's time we went for a tour. I'm sure you're curious to know about the Shadow Lands you saw as you drove in. Why don't I show you their secrets, hmm?"

He turned, and we followed his entourage of armed guards outside to the narrow roadway. On one side, everything was awash in a gray and dead nothingness. On the other, the facility was surrounded by a dense green forest, bursting with life. It was as if someone had laid a filter over the Shadow Lands, turning everything to a monochromatic gray.

King Richard clasped his hands together, the flat

planes of his cheeks brightening in the cool breeze. "I am a curious man by nature. I always wondered what would happen if we brought as many alchemists as we could spare up to our northern border lands, and have them pull as much color as possible." Richard stopped in the center of the empty road. He held his hands wide and smiled. "Of course that was a feat in and of itself. And we wasted a lot of color, which is a shame." He chuckled low. "But the Shadow Lands were the result. They're practically uncrossable by foot, akin to a lifeless desert. The perfect way to protect our border."

So no one could travel further north, neither in nor out. Why would he do that to his own land? Was he crazy? Or was he just willing to make the sacrifices necessary to keep his citizens from making contact with the outside world?

"I'm quite proud of it and plan to expand," he continued. "But that's not really your concern. No, there's more happening here than just changing hundreds of miles of land. Actually, we're conducting some very important experiments. There are things happening at this outpost from which I plan to learn and scale up to our entire kingdom. With your help, we will make New Colony thrive unlike any other nation. The quality of life for our people will rise beyond even your wildest imaginings."

We nodded and a few men clapped. The sound

echoed through the dead land, like a rolling thunder warning of a coming storm.

"I need all my new recruits to understand not only what we're doing and why, but to get on board with it too. I will only have full support from my officers. There are seven of you now, and when the final five of you who are chosen go back to the palace, you will know exactly what is expected of you. You will join our five female recruits and do your duty with zero questions asked. It will be your privilege, and you will be rewarded handsomely."

Calls of "Yes, sir," "Yes, Your Majesty," and "Absolutely" rang out. I said it too, nodding along and smiling like a goon. But something rattled deep in my chest. Skepticism.

The King had the alchemists' magic under his control.

He had the officers.

He had the people.

And with so much opportunity at his fingertips, he'd chosen to utterly devastate countless miles of land without so much as a backward glance. It was maddening to even consider doing something so damaging, but he didn't show an ounce of remorse. If he could do that, what else was he capable of?

I looked around at the hungry faces of my peers. They were ready to do anything asked of them. If they were commanded to do something unimaginable, something wrong, would they do it for their King?

They would—of course they would.

No, the question I should be asking myself wasn't what King Richard was capable of, but rather, what was he capable of making *us* do. Ready or not, I was in this. I was here, one of seven. And I was about to find out just how far I would go for my King.

ELEVEN

The alchemist stood with her back to us, hands outstretched over the poor twiggy shrubs. The green magic swirled around her in colorful tendrils of light, patterns twisting and turning in a trancelike dance. No matter how many times I saw it, alchemy still brought a wave of unease crashing through me. The older alchemist woman was the most skilled I'd seen. She kept pulling from the plants around her, bringing as much of the color inside her as she could, her concentration intense. As she worked her magic, I watched, stunned, as the life, the color, was ripped from the plants, leaving behind a shadow of what once was.

"She's getting *all* the color?" I whispered to Jose, perplexed as to why the King would think this was a good idea. Jose stood still as a statue to my left, body taught as a wire, his frustration equal to my own.

"They're removing all the color they can get. It's the only way to create the Shadow Lands." Reynolds stepped between us. "Whatever they can't get access to, the whites, reds, and blacks, they've found another way to decimate. They burn it."

I shook my head. *And it all just goes to waste?*

Reynolds seemed to read my mind. "It can't be stored. Magic simply gets absorbed and then it's gone forever if it's not applied right away."

"Seems like the Shadow Lands are a waste of valuable resources for a false sense of protection." I clenched my fists, angry with myself for saying as much in front of Reynolds. He worked for the King. He probably supported the project, and if not, had the good sense to keep his mouth shut.

"Careful," was all Reynolds said in reply, nodding to someone approaching.

King Richard.

For the past couple of days we'd learned about what was happening here in the Shadow Lands. The alchemists would touch a plant, pulling the color from it. Instead of using green for healing, or yellow for strength, or whatever else, they would just let it go to waste. It was a slow process, painful to watch. I'd figured out pretty quickly that it took a lot of magic for an alchemist to turn something gray, but there was a whole team of them here, working day and night to finish the job.

I breathed in deep, trying to force the cool morning air to douse my annoyance.

"How's it going over here, Jasmine?" Richard said to the alchemist, a couple of bodyguards trailing close behind him. She turned, her salt-and-pepper braid swinging behind her as the sun danced across her face. She raised a hand to block out the light.

"Well enough," she said. "I think these new officers you got here understand what you're doing with all of this." She raised her eyebrow at me and then winked. I stilled, kicking myself for saying what I had before.

She paused, surveying the damage with thin lips and an intelligent gaze. "Seems to me we're about done here, Your Majesty."

Richard nodded with pride, the buttons of his black suit jacket flashing silver in the sunlight. "Hmm, you may be right. There's really nothing left, is there?" He smiled and patted her on the back.

"Yup. The job is done." She smiled back.

"For now anyway," he said to her. He directed his next comment to us. "We started miles from here and worked our way back to this outpost. Couldn't very well do it the other way around now, could we?" He chuckled. "That land is dead."

The group laughed, and I played along even

though I didn't see what was so funny. The afternoon was the hottest one yet, the sun prickling down its rays on our backs. My mouth watered, and I shifted my weight back and forth between my legs. The stress of trying to be someone I wasn't, of trying to pretend to agree with forever destroying the land, was starting to add to the lightness in my head. I took a deep breath. I needed to get out of here.

"Jasmine," Richard said. "I'd like you to come with me to introduce these men to Francesca."

Jasmine's face drained slightly, her olive skin turning a shade lighter, but she nodded and smiled again. I glanced back at the land, at the scorched horizon, and shuddered. Alchemy was dangerous, that was made clear to me as the days continued. If I was going to really do this, really become a Royal Officer, I needed to be incredibly careful. I couldn't let my guard down, because if these people could kill life so easily, what could they do to me?

I followed our group inside to an enclosed room and was instantly relieved at the blast of air conditioning and the water cooler waiting for us in the corner. I hurried over, gulping down two cups of water before relaxing and turning to take it all in. A row of folding chairs sat against one wall, with a couple set out in the middle of the space. In the far corner a girl stood leaning against the wall, her arms crossed around her small frame. Recognition lit up her eyes when she caught me looking.

I knew this girl.

She had been the one crying that first day I'd gone to the palace. Not Lily, but the younger one. I never did get her name, nor did I see her again.

Until now.

Her hair was styled into two braids down either side of her heart-shaped face, and her blue eyes sparkled with something I couldn't quite put my finger on. Rebelliousness? An unnamed thing that kids her age had—kids on the brink of becoming a teenager, looking at the world like a playground, but not sure if they wanted to play there anymore.

"I'd like you all to meet Francesca," Richard said when the entire group had found our seats.

"It's Frankie," the girl snapped, rolling her large blue eyes.

I rustled in my chair, uncomfortable that this girl was here, that she talked back to royalty like that. What had she said to me? She'd been crying not because someone had hurt her, but because she had hurt *them*.

"That's right." Richard laughed, unperturbed. "I forgot about your snarky little attitude. It's been a few weeks since I've seen you. You're so talented that I overlook the backtalk, don't I? You have it good, little one, because you're the best there is, aren't you?"

She glared, but nodded with a shrug.

He was playing with her emotions, easily manipulating her, and something about that felt utterly wrong. She was a person, a human, but he was acting like she was his to control. Nothing more than a fancy tool.

"Fine, let's get on with it." She sighed, picking a piece of lint from her black shirt and pushing herself off the wall.

"Frankie here," Richard said with a raised eyebrow, "is one of a kind. Wouldn't you say so, Jasmine?"

The old woman stood by the door, her hands clasped behind her back, and nodded. "That's right. She's as unique as they come."

"You see, the thing is," Richard said, "Frankie isn't like the other color alchemists. Frankie has access to a color magic that is newly discovered. For the longest time we've been trying to unravel the secret behind red alchemy. It was always this elusive color no one could seem to do anything with. But little Frankie? She came ready-made with the answer."

Frankie's face flushed crimson. "Who's first?" She asked, cutting off the King's speech and stepping forward. "Do I have any volunteers?"

The urge to help her, to raise my hand, overwhelmed me, but when her eyes connected with mine, I could have sworn I saw her slightly shake her head. I hesitated.

Within seconds, Bryce's hand shot up. "Anything if it pleases you, Your Majesty," he said, completely ignoring Frankie and looking right at King Richard. Bryce was such a suck-up sometimes, but at that moment, I didn't care. Let him stand out in this task. I certainly didn't want to be the first one to figure out what red alchemy did.

The memory of my first meeting with Frankie returned to my mind. I'd asked her if someone was hurting her. She'd laughed. *Nobody's hurting me. Unfortunately it's the other way around.*

"So, should I just take a seat or what?" Bryce asked, standing and pointing to the chairs in the middle of the room.

"Sure," Richard said, a grin slowly stretching across his face. "Frankie, take it away, my dear."

Frankie rolled her eyes again and strode to the other chair. She scraped it against the floor, the metallic legs raw against the concrete, and plopped herself down, glaring at Bryce. He appeared relaxed, that normal smirk playing on his lips, but the tension in his eyes was unmistakable. He was afraid.

"This won't hurt," Frankie said, " ...much."

Quick as a flash, she whipped out a dagger and sliced it across Bryce's bicep. She slapped her hand across the line of blood before he had a moment to react. When he jerked away, horrified, she yelled, "Stop!"

He froze, a bead of sweat rolling down his temple the only visible movement. Somehow transfixed, the tension in his eyes had disappeared, replaced with a glossy sheen. Frankie removed her hand and glanced disgustedly down at the blood on her small palm. Color swirled from it, out into the open air, filtering between her and Bryce, and seeping into them without leaving a mark.

"What's your name?" Frankie asked.

"Bryce," he replied, his tone flat.

"Bryce, do you have a pet at home? A cat or a dog or something?"

"Sparkles." He nodded.

The group laughed nervously, but Bryce was unfazed.

"Who's Sparkles?" Frankie asked, her high voice scratchy.

"My cat."

She clucked her tongue. "I want you to act like Sparkles, please."

Bryce dropped to all fours and moved about the room like a cat—*a freaking cat!* He meowed and arched his back, rubbing against the leg of his now empty chair. Our laughter that followed him was only surface-level; I could practically hear the fear underneath it, it was so thick. All of us were wondering if we were next.

This little girl could control our minds. And we all knew there was nothing we could do to stop her.

Red alchemy wasn't just simple magic, it was dangerous.

Unfortunately, it's the other way around, the girl's original words of warning echoed in my head.

"That's enough," Richard's voice cut through the room. The laughter fizzled out, all eyes back on the King.

"Am I done now?" Frankie asked, folding her arms over her chest and glaring. He nodded, and she stormed from the room. It was obvious that she didn't like her brand of magic, but like everyone, she did it anyway. She did what she was told. Of course she did. The King was in control here, not some little kid. And he had something over everyone, didn't he? I thought of my parents, my mom, our home. What would happen to them if I stepped out of line here?

Richard took us in one by one with his dark shiny eyes and talked slowly. "The Shadow Lands have been my special project for a while now. But Francesca, she is my newest pet. *Our* newest opportunity. I am bound and determined to figure out the secret to expanding this red alchemy." Icy trepidation filled me as I worked to keep my breathing steady, eyes on Richard. "It should be obvious to everyone in this room how valuable red alchemy is." He smiled. Together, we nodded our agreement. "Of course, I would like to have more than one alchemist in this kingdom with this kind of power. And I already deal with a son her age; I could do without the childish drama." The way he spoke of Prince Lucas like that made me bristle. It reminded me of the way my father and I butted heads growing up. It made sense he would want to replicate red alchemy. But how could he if she was so unique? And if he did somehow succeed, what would he do with that power? The implications could be terrible.

"Jasmine is our best healer and leading green alchemist. That's why she's been out here for as long as she has, helping me with the Shadow Lands. But now that we know about Francesca, I've had Jasmine working one-on-one with her, learning about this new gift we've discovered. If anyone can figure out the secret behind Francesca's magic, it would be this one right here." He lifted his hand and nodded respectfully to Jasmine. She smiled and gave a little bow.

"We'll find a way," she assured him. "And as Frankie gets older, we will be able to mold her into what she needs to be."

"That much is true," Richard replied. "Now, Reynolds. What do you think of all of this?"

Silence stretched through the room as we recruits turned toward our leader.

"It's brilliant." Reynolds stood, his grin sheepish—something I'd never seen on him before. "I'd love to be part of it. As I'm sure these boys will as well."

The King's eyes were alight with excitement. He nodded, raking a hand through his hair.

"Me–oow," Bryce—*or should I say Sparkles*—purred from the corner. He shook, his eyes going wild, seemingly aware that something had gone wrong, but he couldn't control himself. He was still a cat, and I still had to hold back my laughter.

I *almost* felt bad for the guy.

Richard grinned. "I guess I should have told Francesca to make him stop that behavior." He pointed to one of the bodyguards standing beside him. "Go get her, will you?" He chuckled to himself, enjoying every bit of Bryce's humiliation. "She needs to remember to clean up her messes."

"Speaking of which." Jasmine pointed to Bryce's cut, now dripping into a pool of blood on the floor. She strode to him, kneeled, and pulled a wad of leaves from her pocket, healing his wound with green alchemy. The magic fascinated me, a soothing balm beyond medical reason.

"Don't worry about your friend," Richard said. "He'll be fine, and he'll remember the whole thing.

Probably won't be volunteering for that again anytime soon."

My eyes remained on the green magic happening in the corner of the room between Jasmine and Bryce. I blinked a few times before dragging my focus back to the King.

Richard stood in the doorway, ready to leave. He paused for a long second, and then turned back to Reynolds. "Considering what your boys have seen, and the plans I have for New Colony, I've decided I need more than just five new Royal Officers in this year's class. I will take all seven of them."

He swept from the room, the door slamming with a finalizing echo.

We turned to one another, dumbfounded. Had that really just happened?

"Congratulations, boys," Reynolds growled, his thin mouth moving into a sinister smile. "Welcome to the family. There's no turning back now."

TWELVE

I woke in a panic. My throat ached for water, the sheets plastered to my body. I gripped the edges of the bed and sat up, catching my breath in gasps of thick air. The darkness wrapped around me, the small room empty and silent except for my own pleading heartbeat.

How had I ended up here? This job, this Royal Officer thing—it wasn't what I wanted. I should have sabotaged this stupid training long ago. I'd known it wasn't anything good, not anything I wanted to be involved with, but I'd hesitated. And now I was in deep. The King wanted me, he wanted all of us. I couldn't very well back out now, not with what I knew. I was privy to secrets an outsider would never be permitted to have.

First the Shadow Lands.

Now, red alchemy.

It was all too much.

I yanked off the blankets and stumbled from the bed.

I couldn't breathe.

Get me out of here. I need out!

It wasn't like I could just run away, but at the very least, I needed to be outside so I could breathe and think and calm my racing heart. I needed the night's fresh air to fill my lungs. Only then would I be able to think clearly again. My panic still clung to me, and I forced myself to keep moving away from my bunk.

It was the middle of the night, silent as death.

I walked as softly across the polished concrete floor as I could manage. King Richard would have his guards posted near his sleeping quarters, so I headed in the opposite direction. Down the set of stairs and out the closest door, the one next to the Shadow Lands. I nearly cried out when the cool air washed over me; it felt so good.

"Everything is going to be okay," I whispered aloud to myself, trying to make myself believe the words.

Nobody liked being over on this side of the building. It was all the dead land, and it was creepy as hell. The other officers stationed out here avoided it like it was contagious. Jasmine and Frankie were the only alchemists still left at this place, and they were inside asleep. Out here, I could be alone. I could think. I just needed to be quiet, to stay hidden. I breathed in deep and closed my eyes for a long second.

So think, Tristan. How on earth are you going to get yourself out of this one?

Snapping my eyes open, I strolled out onto the road, looking up at the night sky. The stars glowed bright and unlimited, a kaleidoscope of something without a name. Freedom. But more than freedom.

And I was nothing but a speck of a man stuck down here to live out my fate.

Something cracked nearby and I froze.

Again, the crackling sound sliced through the night, echoing over the barren roadway. Someone was coming from around the building, their boots crunching on the gravel.

Instinct took over, and I ran as silently as possible to the cover of the Shadow Lands. The gray, dead trees were my only hiding place and I wasn't about to let my fear of them stop me. I jumped behind the nearest one and stood motionless against its thick, scratchy trunk, holding my breath.

"This way," someone said low, and footsteps crossed the pavement.

I stilled, listening for more, praying I blended in, that darkness would be ample cover.

"Come in here," a woman's voice replied. "No one would know to look for us here."

Then two figures stumbled into the brush only feet away, their backs turned from me.

"Do you have blue on you?" the deeper voice asked.

"I couldn't get any," the woman replied. "But there are no blue alchemists here to eavesdrop on us anyway, we should be fine." Then she shifted slightly toward me and my entire body prickled with shock, seeing enough of her through the thicket of branches to identify her.

Jasmine.

"We're alone out here?" the other voice pressed in a low and haughty whisper. "We can talk openly? We're safe?" Something about that voice was familiar. I frowned. Could it be?

"When are we ever safe," she replied flatly. "But we're as alone as we're going to get. Let's just be quick about it."

"Alright," he replied. "I hate this."

"Me too, but it's our life." She paused. "Are you still sure you're ready to run away from it all, from New Colony?" she asked the broad-shouldered man who I still couldn't see but was starting to have a pretty good idea about his identity. He nodded and pulled her in for a hug. "If you get caught, you'll be hanged for treason," she continued, voice growing thick with emotion.

"This is the plan, Jas. I have to go through with it. But I'll be alright," he muttered, his head resting on the top of hers. "It's you who I'm worried about. I still think you should come with me. This has gotten out of hand. You shouldn't be around that lunatic any longer."

Then the man shifted his face toward me and my suspicions were confirmed, even if I could hardly believe it was true. I stepped back, my boot crunching on a fallen tree branch. I cursed to myself. Like an idiot, I'd let my surprise reveal my location and identity. They both spun toward me in an instant, guards up and ready to fight.

"It's okay," I croaked, carefully stepping forward from the thicket of trees. "It's just me, Tristan."

There was a long pause as they scrutinized me. Finally, the man stepped forward, the moonlight lighting his face. It was Officer Reynolds.

"Are you alone?" he asked, his voice turning deadly. He was going to kill me, wasn't he?

"Yes," I said quickly. "I'm alone, I swear." I held up my hands. "Please don't hurt me."

"He's a spy," Jasmine spat.

"No," I replied, fear bubbling to the surface. My eyes flicked to where I knew Reynolds had a gun on his hip. It would be so easy for them to kill me and make up some story to cover for it. "I swear, I just came out here to get some air and when I heard you two coming I got spooked and hid. I never meant to spy on you. I'm not a spy. I swear it."

I could barely make out their complete expressions in the darkness, but I was pretty sure she was scowling in disbelief while Reynolds was smiling. A warm sense of relief washed through me. "I believe him," Reynolds said. "He's a good kid. I think we can trust him. He's not been keen on this training since day one."

Jasmine relaxed slightly, but still eyed me with distrust. I didn't blame her. I wouldn't trust me either if I were in her shoes.

"You're running away?" I questioned Reynolds.

He looked away, but I knew it was true. He was. "Please," I said, "please, take me with you. I want nothing to do with whatever King Richard has planned. I need out."

"You'll only slow him down," Jasmine said. "We need Reynolds to be successful."

There are more of them? Who was this "we" she was referring to? I wanted to ask the questions so badly, but I made myself stay focused.

"No," I said. "I'm strong, fast, and I want to do what's right. I can help him with whatever he needs.

Just get me out of here, because this," I pointed around us, "is wrong."

They looked to each other for a long moment, seeming to consider my offer.

"Reynolds, sir," I said, "with all due respect, the King is a madman. I can't work for him. You're my only option."

"What if you went home?" Jasmine whispered the question, a reminder to us all that we needed to be quick.

"I've seen too much. The King would never allow me to go home and you know it." I paused. "Besides, there's not much to go back to. My father isn't much better than Richard."

"Todd?" Reynolds shook his head. "No, Todd is a good man. Solid character. I've known him for years."

"He's not," I said. "You can't trust him. Whatever you're trying to do here, don't trust my father with any of it." I shook, my hands fisted, angry tears forming in my traitorous eyes. "He beat me, okay? He treated me like a punching bag for years; why do you think I ended up at the warehouse in the first place? I was learning to box so I could defend myself at home."

They stood motionless, staring at me with mouths agape.

I looked away. "It's over now. Just please, don't make me go back there, not home and not to that horrible palace. Take me with you." I was going to cry. Hot tears threatened to escape and I hated myself for it.

Unexpectedly, Reynolds advanced and wrapped me into a tight hug. I froze, unable to recall the last time someone had hugged me. The warmth enveloped me like a blanket. I tried to hold back the tears, feeling like such a child, but they came anyway. My shoulders began to shake. But he didn't move, didn't call out my weakness, and a slow relief washed through me like warm honey.

I was done with that life. Done with my father. Done with the alchemists and the officers and all of it. I needed to start fresh, away from the pain. I needed a chance to be me—the me underneath all this extra guilt.

"Please, take me with you," I whispered one more time, my face pressed against Reynolds' broad shoulder. It sounded like the plea of a desperate man. It *was* the plea of a desperate man.

"Okay, Tristan," he finally said, his voice low. "Let's get out of here. You can come with me. But are you absolutely sure this is what you want? Once we leave, you can never come back."

I swallowed hard and he released me. I wrapped my arms around myself. This decision couldn't be undone. It was final. But I knew that I needed to take it. I had to believe fate had led me here tonight. This was my chance to leave New Colony and start over. If I stayed, who knew what terrors I'd endure.

"I'm sure," I said.

He sighed. "Okay, but we have to leave tonight."

I nodded, ignoring the rush of panic. "Thank you," my voice cracked. "I won't let you down."

THIRTEEN

We crept along the back of the building, the plan replaying over and over in my mind. I combed through it, looking for holes. *Oh, there were holes all right, obvious problems.*

But this was my one chance and I wasn't about to back down now.

"The royal helicopter is already on the roof and we have a pilot who's on our side. He's agreed to go north with Reynolds. I'm sure it will be fine to pop you in there too," Jasmine had said as we'd fleshed out the plan back in the dead forest. She would be staying behind, a spy in Richard's network and a key player for the Resistance. "It's past two in the morning now, the pilot has agreed to meet us at three, but we need to get moving. The next guard shift-change is at four, so we need to get you men out of here before those guards start to wake up. There's no one up on the roof, but they do sit outside Richard's door. Hopefully the two currently on duty will have fallen asleep by now."

I doubted it. But I made myself believe in the plan anyway.

I hoped it would be enough.

It had to be.

We opened the door to the stairwell and began to climb the narrow, metal staircase, keeping as quiet as possible. It was darker in here than outside, the overhead lights switched off for the night. Good thing.

"If anyone stops us," Reynolds whispered, "just follow my lead, okay?"

Jasmine nodded, dark shadows playing across her face as we moved.

"Okay, Officer Reynolds," I whispered back.

"Once we're out of here, just call me Hank, you got that, kid?"

I nodded, a smile creeping at my lips. *Hank, huh?* It fit him.

As we ascended the four-story building, I glanced through the glass doors on each floor, taking in the last of what I'd ever see of this horrible place.

Floor one was administrative.

Floor two had the room where Bryce had become Sparkles. Okay, now *that* I did not want to forget, the one highlight of my stay here.

Floor three housed the dormitory rooms where many of my new friends lay asleep in their beds. I pushed down momentary regret, knowing they would never see me again, wishing I could take some of them with me.

Jasmine turned on us, her eyes glossy pools in the darkness. "This is my stop. It's also where Frankie and the King are staying as well." She peered through the window for a second, her mouth pinching.

"Won't the guards see you?" I whispered back, my body prickling with concern. If she was caught, we'd all be exposed.

"They should be around the corner," she assured me, her raspy voice barely above a whisper. "If they catch me, trust me, they're scared of alchemists. They won't stop to question me, and if they do, I'll be able to cover for you. But no matter what happens to me, you two need to keep moving."

Frankie.

The thought of the girl brought a knife of guilt slashing through me. I stopped, knowing what I had to ask. Also knowing I couldn't ask it because they'd never agree.

Do it anyway. Do the right thing.

"Wait," I said, blowing out a breath. "We've got to take Frankie with us."

"What?" Reynolds shot back, his voice tight. "No,

that's crazy. She's Richard's most valuable asset. He'll never let her get away."

I shook my head, careful to keep my voice down. "She's a good person. She doesn't want to be here anymore than you or I do. And if we can get her out of here, we can slow Richard's plans down because he won't have her red alchemy anymore."

"It's too risky," Reynolds said, but his voice had slowed to thoughtfulness and I knew he was starting to consider my suggestion. "She's too powerful. What if she doesn't want to go with us? No, forget it. We're running late as it is. We need to get to the roof and meet the pilot."

But I couldn't. I'd left my mom. I'd left my best friends back home. I was about to leave the only friends I'd made here. I wasn't perfect, wasn't always a good person, but this was my chance to do something right. I could make a difference. I'd seen the way Frankie was treated like an object, seen the tears in her eyes, the defiance in her stance. She reminded me so much of myself. My mind raced back to the day I'd met her and what Lily had said, that I needed to get through training so that I could save a girl. Maybe Frankie was that girl.

Either way, I couldn't leave the girl behind.

"I have to try," I said, my mind made up.

"I think he's right," Jasmine whispered, finally

adding her opinion to the conversation. She peered through the window in the door again, then turned back to us, her face tired but her eyes alert. "Frankie doesn't want to be here. But I also think Hank is right, too." She leveled her gaze on me, and even though it was dark, I could see the apprehension there. "It's risky. We shouldn't deviate from the plan."

"Screw the plan," I hissed between gritted teeth. "You head up, I'll get Frankie, and we'll meet you there in a couple of minutes."

I pushed past Jasmine and through the door, mentally throwing the plan out the window. Careful to keep my movements silent, I pushed down the mounting fear and searched for signs of Francesca.

"You don't even know where she's staying." Jasmine slid next to me, her voice barely audible. She pointed to an unmarked door. "It's locked from the outside and you don't have the key," she said, gently placing her hand against it. The deadbolt clicked out of place.

"How did you...?" I looked around, my voice trailing off. We were still alone, but what had Jasmine said? King Richard's guards were just around the corner and more would be switching patrols soon. We needed to hurry.

"Simple, yellow alchemy." She sighed quietly, her hand wrapped around her necklace. "Be careful," she said. "I'll go distract the guards by Richard's room so they don't come over here. If Frankie resists, tell her I said to trust you, and if she still resists, leave her and go to the roof anyway."

I was suddenly reminded of the day my father walked into that warehouse and put my life on a different path. He thought he was helping me. If only he knew, what would he say about me now? No matter. That part of my life was over. And now I was about to change this girl's life. I hoped I wasn't making a mistake.

Slowly, I opened the door and quickly closed it behind me. It clicked into place and I turned to face the little bedroom.

Frankie was already sitting up. Her white nightgown shone in the moonlight from the window behind her, her hair loose, her small face filled with bewilderment. It quickly transformed to pure rage.

"Do you want to die today or are you just as stupid as you look?" she spat, her voice dripping with the threat of death.

I swallowed hard, lifting my hands. A trickle of fear ran through me. Never had I considered that she'd kill me for coming in her room. But she was the most powerful alchemist in the kingdom and what was I? I had no gun. I had no authority. No magic. Nothing.

FOURTEEN

"What's your name again?" She tilted her head, her glare piercing. For a young girl, she had more anger in her than anyone I'd ever met. "Tristan, right? You can't be here, *Tristan*. Haven't you heard? I do bad things to people."

"I'm sorry," I said, pressing myself to the door and trying to keep my voice down. What had I gotten myself into? This girl wasn't just a victim in need of saving; she was a downright creepy terror who could make me do anything she wanted. She sat on her bed, a ghostly white image in a small dark room. There were bars on her window. The door had been locked from the outside in. This might as well be a prison cell. But to keep others out, or to keep her in?

"You have no idea what sorry even means," she snapped, fisting the sheets in her hands and shifting to her knees. At any moment, she could spring on me, draw blood, and all of this would be over.

A terrible situation had turned her into some kind of monster, but despite that, I wanted to help her. I saw my younger self in her now more than ever. I saw that anger, that desperation, that deep, deep sadness. This girl was me five years ago, and I'd be damned to leave her here.

"Jasmine told me to tell you that you can trust me. I don't have time to explain everything in detail," I said in a rush, "but if you want out of this place, if you want to get away from King Richard and New Colony, I can help you do that." I swallowed hard, hoping she'd be able to see me as someone here to help her and not hurt her. This was a girl who was used to being hurt, being used. And even now, her expression stayed in its defensive state. "Thing is," I continued, "you're going to have to trust me and come with me *right now*."

Slowly, she stepped out of the bed, her white nightgown falling around her knobby knees, and stood. "Why should I believe you?"

We didn't have time. But this girl deserved freedom more than anyone I'd met. She was more a prisoner than I'd ever be, what with her power being what it was. "I know what it feels like," I said, "to have someone control your life, someone nasty and hateful."

"Yeah right." Her eyes narrowed to slits. "You have no idea what I've been through, what I've *done*."

"Okay, fair enough," I replied, giving into a moment of vulnerability. "But my dad is a total dick-wad, so maybe I know a little bit about it." Surprisingly, she giggled, her whole demeanor softening for a split second before she returned to her lioness-like stance.

"Anyway, he beat me up, every chance he got, and when I was younger, if someone had a way to get me away from him, I'd have jumped at the chance."

She scrutinized me, biting her lower lip, but her eyes had softened and her stance was starting to thaw. This was it.

"This is your chance, Frankie," I said, stepping toward her despite the danger. "Either take it or leave it. But I'd like you to take it. I'd like to help you."

She paused for a second, peering around the small bedroom, then slowly, she nodded. "Okay," she said in a sure voice. She walked to the corner of the room and slipped her small feet into black sandals, then opened a dresser drawer and pulled out a black jacket. "Let's go." She smiled at me, and it was the first time I'd ever seen her do that. It was shocking, so bright and open and contagious and great. I smiled back, relieved. There was hope for this kid.

Tentatively, I opened the door and we slipped

outside. Voices talked low from around the corner and the velvet laugh of a woman danced down the hallway.

"I better get to bed," I heard Jasmine say. "Thanks for the chat, guys. I needed a good laugh."

I grabbed Frankie's hand and tugged her forward to the stairwell entrance. Glancing through the glass to make sure it was clear, I looked back at her and nodded. I opened the door and we slid through, carefully closing the door behind us. This was easy, almost too easy. Not one guard had seen me all night. It was only a matter of time before my luck ran out. My senses pricked up and urgency propelled me up the stairs.

"We're going to the roof?" Frankie whispered.

I nodded and held my finger to my lips. She nodded back and, being the brave kid she was, rushed in front of me to lead the way. Just as we reached the next landing up, a door opened and shut below us. Footsteps thumped on the metal stairs, one floor down, and we both froze. Nervous energy swirled around us as we pushed ourselves against the wall. Frankie's stance mimicked mine, cautious, but ready to fight if needed. If there was anyone who could stand up for herself, it was this kid. And I felt guilty for even thinking that because she *was* just a kid.

"I hate this shift," a man's weary voice echoed from

the stairs below. "Nobody in their right mind can be fully alert this early in the morning."

Another man chuckled. "Oh, don't be such a baby."

I waited for them to come up the stairs, to discover us, pull their guns and shoot, but the door opened and shut again. They were gone.

Relief seeped through me and I closed my eyes for a second, trying to still not only my mind, but my trembling body as well. That had been too close. How long until they realized what was going on? How long until I was executed for treason?

"This is it," Frankie whispered, grin lighting up her face again. She reached for the handle of the thick door and pulled it open with the slight grind of metal on metal.

Together, we stepped out onto the roof.

The slight breeze brushed over me, hinting at something I'd never had before: freedom. It was still dark out, but the moon was higher in the sky and my eyes had adjusted so much that I could easily make out the helicopter waiting for us. Hank Reynolds stood with another man who I assumed to be the pilot. They must have been waiting for us. I swallowed hard, shaking out my hands. Thank God, I was more than ready to get out of here.

"I got her," I said, moving in closer to our crew. "We're free to go now."

The whites of Hank's eyes flashed toward me and his mouth turned down into a deep grimace. I stiffened, the moment stretching with heightened awareness. Something was terribly wrong.

"Oh, freedom, huh?" Bryce sauntered out from the shadows, holding up a gun. "Really, this is almost comical. You're making it easy for me, Tristan. You're such a screw-up, aren't you?"

I shoved Frankie behind me and glared, anger and sickly fear filling my mouth, tasting of copper. "What are you doing here?" I asked.

It was a stupid question, but I had to stall. Of all the people who could have caught me up here, Bryce was the worst. The guy hated me, and this was his perfect chance to kill me. From the look on his face, he knew it too. He leveled the gun, pointing it right at me. His smile was calculated wickedness. I didn't stand a chance.

FIFTEEN

"You're not as sneaky as you think you are, Tristan," Bryce jeered with a sickening laugh. "Isn't that right, Jose?"

"I think that's a fair assessment," Jose said as he came around from the back of the helicopter. He rubbed the back of his head, a sour expression on his face. He looked tired, worried. Betrayed. And the sight of him doubled my panic. He sidled up behind Hank and the pilot, a gun pointed at them as well. My gaze flicked to the two men's waists, noting the weapons missing from their holsters. They must have been caught off guard and overtaken by the two recruits.

"You don't know what you're doing," I said, ignoring Jose for now and focusing on Bryce. "Put the gun down. You don't want to do this."

"You always thought you were better than me."

Bryce's brown eyes and dirty blond hair were barely distinguishable across the darkness, but I could picture his anger just the same. "Why do you think I went to your father in the first place, huh? Someone had to take you down a notch. But even then, you got to be the shining star. Always Horace's favorite and now Reynolds too. Well, not anymore!"

I blinked, taking in the information. Bryce had been the one to tell my father about the fighting. That was probably why he'd been spared and allowed to come to this training as well, some kind of deal with the devil.

How had I missed it? It was so obvious now. Bryce had let all those men back at our boxing club pay for his leg up in life. My stomach churned; I was so angry.

"Just put the gun down," I continued to try to defuse him, hopeless as it was. "This isn't what you think. You don't understand."

"Don't I? You're running off like a scared little hypocrite, taking that *thing*," he glared at Francesca, "with you. Where are you going, anyway?"

I felt Frankie bristle behind me, felt her need to pounce. "Easy," I whispered, continuing to block her way forward.

"Bryce." I shook my head. "I don't have a problem with you, and whatever this is about, you're making a mistake."

"Son, put the gun down and we can explain," Reynolds spoke up, stepping slightly forward with his hands raised.

"Shut up, old man! You're going to be my prize when I turn you in to King Richard for whatever treasonous plan you've cooked up here."

I looked to Jose, his eyes round and shocked. At first I'd assumed Jose was in on this with Bryce, but now I wasn't so sure. Maybe he'd been dragged into this. He had a gun, too. Bryce wasn't going to see reason, but Jose? He was so different than Bryce.

"This is Frankie, remember?" I peered over at Jose, leveling my gaze on him. I hated to bring her into this, but Jose had a soft heart. He'd been *concerned* about the alchemists from day one, even if he tried to hide it.

"Get that little brat away from me." Bryce spat on the ground.

"I first met Frankie in the palace," I continued talking only to Jose. "She was so young, and she was crying and crying over what she was being forced to do to other people. She was hiding out with this woman, a purple alchemist who's about our age. And this woman, Lily, she was so tired. You should have seen her, Jose. She's literally being worked to death."

"Lily?" Jose's stoic veneer crumbled and his voice came out raw. "You met Lily?"

"Shut up," Bryce growled, waving his gun around. "I'm in charge here!"

"No, this isn't about *you*," Jose spat, turning his attention on Bryce, his normally cool self-composure completely abandoned. "Lily was my best friend growing up until they took her away. That's why I'm here, why I applied to this stupid program three years in a row, just so I could find her again."

Bryce stalked toward Jose, his gun still being carelessly tossed around as he waved his hands about. "You're pathetic! You know that? You came here searching for a *girl*?" His laugh was a disgusted sneer. "You're no better than Tristan."

I looked between them, my heart racing with opportunity. Bryce and Jose were on one side of the helicopter landing pad and the rest of us were now on the other. Reynolds caught my expression and narrowed his eyes, nodding slightly. Beside him, the helicopter pilot still stood silent, a thin man with a shiny bald head and sharp eyes glaring daggers at Bryce. Frankie stayed behind me, feet planted in place. It was four against one on our end. But what about Jose?

"Lily needs you, Jose," Hank Reynolds spoke up again. "She needs you, just like Frankie needs our help tonight. Do you understand?"

Jose broke from his argument with Bryce and nodded once at Reynolds.

"Seriously," Bryce shouted, pointing his gun on Hank. "Shut up when I tell you to shut—"

Jose pushed Bryce. The gun slipped from his hand and slid across the ground. A split second later, Reynolds dove onto the gun and jumped to his feet, pointing the weapon at Bryce.

"Let's go," he barked toward Frankie and me. "Now!" We wasted no time, racing toward the helicopter.

Bryce cussed and jumped to his feet, making a grab at Frankie. He caught her by the wrist and tugged her back against his chest.

"Wrong move, buddy!" she snapped, clawing at his face.

"No!" Bryce yelped, realizing too late that she'd drawn blood. Frankie had a hold of him and there was nothing he could do about it now, not with her level of magic.

"Get as far away from me, as fast as possible, right this instant!" she cried out in a torrent of emotion.

And he did.

Bryce dashed from Frankie, right to the edge of the roof and jumped. Moments later, a terrible thud pierced the night.

Frankie screamed. Shock burned through my body,

my stomach flopping violently. I froze to the spot, unable to go look. But Reynolds rushed to the edge of the building and peered over. Turning back, he gave us a quick shake of his head. "He's dead."

"Oh my God," Jose's voice was hollow, the color leaching from his face.

"I didn't mean to." Frankie's eyes were wide. "I swear it."

"We know," Reynolds said, hurrying toward us. "We all heard you. You couldn't have known that's how he would react. But you screamed pretty loud and it won't be long until someone comes up here to investigate. We have to go. Now."

"I'm out of here," Jose said. "Sorry, but I have to help Lily." He shook his head sharply and rushed toward the door.

"What is wrong with me?" Frankie cried, falling to a heap on the floor. "That's not the first time it's happened, you know?" She sobbed. "I'm evil. I'm a bad person. I–I–I can't help it."

"It's not your fault," I said, lifting her into my arms, not allowing myself to fear her or her alchemy for a second. Yes, she was dangerous. Yes, she could kill. But she didn't mean to, and she didn't want to. She was still a child, and more than anything, she needed to get out of this place. She needed to be free. "But right now, we have to get out of here."

"Let's go." The pilot threw open the door to the chopper and we all climbed inside. He began to flip switches and the machine buzzed to life. "Strap in, we've made a lot of commotion," he yelled back. "Hang on tight. We'll be followed and we might not make it out of New Colony alive."

I gulped, swallowing down my fear, and flattened myself against the boxy seat. Seconds later, the helicopter ascended into the dark sky. The sound of the rudders created such a loud rumble, there was no doubt our escape would be discovered almost instantly.

Metal dinged on metal and the chopper dipped. Bullets.

"Stay low!" The pilot yelled, veering us to the right. More bullets rained in our direction, and I squeezed my eyes shut for a second before opening them to find Frankie staring back, fear shining behind watery blue tears.

"It's okay," I said, "We're going to be okay. I've got you."

She nodded and then looked out the window. I joined her to squint into the darkness. There appeared to be Royal Officers on the rooftop, shiny black guns drawn and firing in our direction. But we flew faster and they got smaller with each passing second. We couldn't be stopped now.

I released a deep sigh of relief, hope flickering to

life inside me like never before. We were doing it. We were getting out. I regretted leaving my friends behind, leaving my mother, knowing that I'd never see them again, but this was the right thing to do, not only for my future, but for the future of New Colony. I would make the Resistance proud. I would take this chance to be my own man and prove myself worthy.

Below us, the military building faded into the distance. I squinted, wondering if what I was seeing was real or my imagination. It appeared as though none other than King Richard was stumbling across the rooftop, hands outstretched and pointing right toward us. But we were too far away to say for sure that it was him, and seconds later, the inky night bled through the scene, shrouding us in complete darkness.

SEVEN YEARS LATER - FRANKIE

"I'm so bored," I grumbled. "Seriously, Tristan, if you don't do something to entertain me, I'm going to die."

We sat on his couch, my head resting against his shoulder and my bare feet tucked under my bum. I casually tossed the paperback book down to the floor and peered up at him, fluttering my lashes like an idiot.

"What do you want me to do?" He never took his eyes off of his own book. Go figure.

"I dunno, that's *your* job to figure out."

He shook his head and turned the page. *Traitor*.

Truth was, reading was something we'd grown fond of out here at camp. After we'd run away with Hank years ago, we'd set up our new home, welcoming in strangers as they came to us. They came often. Our networks had grown. We had people specially trained to transport New Colony's rejects up to us. I lived in a cabin with a bunch of other single young women, but Tristan had built himself his own cabin.

He was such a show off sometimes.

"Oh, I know," I purred. "Why don't you tell me a joke?"

He always was so funny, making light of every-thing. Not that he used to be that way. When I'd first met him, he'd been a brooding teenager with a past almost as dark as mine. But over the years, he'd light-ened up and transformed into the kind of guy who smiled all the time. And wow, what a smile that boy had. It was a gift, really, something that I loved about my best friend. His optimism came naturally these days, though he liked to remind me it wasn't actually natural, but a result of gaining his freedom and meeting me.

"Why did the cucumber blush?" he asked, putting his book down and turning that hundred-watt grin on me. My eyes flicked to his lips. What? I couldn't help it.

"Why?" I asked, raising a curious eyebrow.

"Because he saw the salad dressing."

I paused, and then rolled my eyes in exasperation. That was just about the dumbest joke I'd ever heard.

"Come on," he said with a playful shrug, "it's a little funny."

"You're so cute when you try hard," I teased, then tickled his side.

"Oh no you don't." He retaliated, pinning me to the couch in an instant, his body heavy over mine, leaving me no choice but to surrender. We'd agreed long ago that I wouldn't use my alchemy on him, so this wasn't a fair fight. I was quite short, much to my dismay, but had filled out well, and my recent shoulder-length haircut made me feel more mature. He, on the other hand, had turned into a gorgeous twenty-four-year-old man. But still my Tristan though; the boy who'd saved me that dark night seven years ago.

He tickled my side, and I let out a shriek. "I give up!"

"You're such a dork," he said, rolling off me.

"Ha! You're the one who just told a joke about salad dressing."

"You loved it." He smiled cheekily.

I did, but he didn't have to know that. Lately I'd been thinking maybe I loved *him*. I'd dated a few other guys in camp, but nobody even came remotely close to Tristan. He was funny, kind, smart, attractive, and well, he was *my* person.

But I was terrified of telling him, positive he didn't feel the same way about me, always treating me like a sister. I was sure he thought I was too young for him. And for years, I had been. But I'd grown up too.

"I know, let's go swimming," he said. "It's getting stuffy in here."

I was more of a homebody than he was. I could holed up for hours in this cabin, but he liked to get outside as much as possible. We'd go hiking, fishing, and swimming in the summer. The winters were a lot harder up here in this cold Canadian forest, but we had Resistance business to deal with anyway, so we always had something to keep us occupied.

"Swimming sounds great," I said, "and somehow, I knew you'd want to go swimming today." I laughed and lifted the hem of my shirt to flash my dark blue one-piece.

He raised an eyebrow, a blush creeping across his tanned cheeks. Oh goodness, he was so cute, and he didn't even know it. I loved how different he looked from me. I was short, blonde, blue-eyed, and curvy. For years I'd been gangly, but not anymore, thank goodness. I finally felt like a grown woman. He was tall, broad, and his half-Asian heritage had given him that sexy dark look that drove the girls crazy. Me included.

Seriously, I had it bad.

"You know you're the best, right?" He took a small step back. "I really appreciate our friendship." His smile was slightly awkward as he reached into his drawer to grab his swim trunks. "Okay, one second." He strode into his bathroom and shut the door.

"No, you're the best," I whispered, embarrassment rushing through me. *I really appreciate our friendship? What does that mean?*

Not what I wanted it to.

He wanted to *stay* friends. Nothing more.

I needed to forget this crush, at least for now. The last thing I wanted was for Tristan to push me away. I didn't have anyone else. Well, except for Hank, but that was different. Hank was more of a mentor. Tristan was... everything else.

"Knock, knock," said a voice I knew well as he tapped on Tristan's door.

Speaking of Hank...

"We're in here," I called, and Hank let himself in.

"What's going on?" he asked, coming to give me a quick hug. He was a hugger, that Hank. Dressed in burley clothes and sporting a scraggly beard, Hank fit right in with the forest landscape. Our very own lumberjack! His kind eyes wrinkled around the edges when he smiled at me. He was getting older. We all were. I sighed.

Tristan came out of the bathroom, his trunks low on his hips. "We're going swimming. Wanna come?" *Oh heavens, keep your eyes up, Frankie. And close your mouth!*

"I need to talk to you guys," Hank said, letting out a

breath and turning serious. "It's important. Is now a good time?"

"Good a time as any," Tristan replied and I nodded, worry rising in my chest.

"What's going on?" I asked.

"Well, as you know we've been waiting for an opportunity to get another one of our people back in New Colony, right?" Hank leaned against the wall, folding his arms. "We need to plant a spy."

"Yes," I replied. A little surge of excitement raced through me. "Did you figure something out?" If he did, it would be a game changer for us.

"Thing is," Hank said slowly, as if it pained him to say it aloud, "I've been in communication with Jasmine, and things are getting pretty bad at the palace. She wants someone who can make it out there to work with her."

"Like an officer?" I asked.

He cocked his head and narrowed his eyes.

"No," Tristan said sharply. "No way."

Did they want Tristan to go? That would be suicide. He couldn't go back there! He'd be recognized in an instant. He'd met the King when he was sixteen, and he had changed, but not *that* much.

"Yeah, there's no way Tristan can get back inside unnoticed." I shrugged. "Sorry."

They both turned to me, expressions grim. Anger

flashed across Tristan's face, and Hank's was the picture of guilt. What the heck?

"He wasn't talking about me," Tristan growled, balling his hand into a fist and punched the wall. Shock raced through me. I'd never seen him to do anything like that before. *It was solid wood, after all!* He glared at Hank as he cradled his injured hand.

I rushed forward, reaching for him. "Tristan! Are you okay? Can I help?" A little green alchemy and he'd be good as new.

"I have to go," he said, storming out of the cabin and slamming the door behind him.

I stood there, frozen and perplexed. The Tristan I knew *rarely* got angry.

Hank met my gaze and edged closer, putting an arm around my shoulder. "The thing is, Frankie, Jasmine needs another alchemist." He frowned, and I shook my head, the realization of what was happening hitting me like an arrow. I pushed away from him. "You're the best one for the job," he pressed on. "You haven't been in the kingdom since you were a kid, you've grown up and look very different now, and you're incredibly talented with magic. We need your help."

"But I don't do red alchemy anymore!" It was true. "So if that's what you think this is about, you can forget it." I'd blocked the red after killing Bryce that night;

somehow the trauma had allowed me to shove the ability down into the recesses of my mind. Denial at its finest! Or at least, that's the way I liked to joke about it with Tristan.

"I know, and you won't have to do red again, don't worry," he said, his voice as earnest as I'd ever heard it. I forced myself to calm down before I turned back to him. They needed me? Was he certain it had to be me? "We've already created a false identity for you and got you all logged into the system. You'll be known as an alchemist named Sasha, and will spend some time at an outpost like the one we saved you from. Then, when the time is right, you'll move into the palace to help Jasmine."

"I can't believe this is happening," I sputtered, my hands beginning to shake as I realized this thing was actually going to happen. "I don't want to leave Tristan. Or you."

Hank nodded, his face softening just before he pulled me into another hug. He towered over me, making me feel all the more vulnerable. Would I be able to survive New Colony again? Just the idea of it made me want to barf! "I know," he said in understanding. "We'll miss you, kid. But it's not forever. And it could save a lot of people. Think about that, think about your family back there."

"My family?" I barked, peeling away from him and

beyond frustrated. "Trust me, they don't think about me."

I stood and ran my fingers through my thick hair.

"Just think about it, okay?" Hank asked. "I'm asking this of you only because you're needed. Remember what we're doing in the first place. We can only survive out here if they can survive in there. The Resistance has to come first sometimes, as much as I hate that fact about our life, it's true."

"Fine," I whispered, meeting his eyes through blurred vision. He was right. Of course he was right—he was Hank. "I'll think about it." But even as I said the words, I knew I would agree. I was committed to the Resistance.

I left him in the cabin and raced down to the lake, the camp flashing past me in a blur of log cabins and pine trees and people milling about.

Once I got to the lake's edge, I found Tristan floated in the middle, staring up at the cloudless sky. I pulled off my shirt and shorts and ran in, swimming to him as fast as I could.

"Hey," I said, sputtering water.

"Hi," he replied stiffly, still floating.

"Will you talk to me about this or do I need to dunk you first?"

He laughed but it felt forced, and then he righted himself. We swam to where we could stand, the water lapping against our chins. I would miss this. Miss the hot summer sun beating down on our shoulders, miss the smell of pine and lake water, miss *him*.

"You're going to go, aren't you?" He moved in close, rubbing his hands up and down my arms. I nodded, and watched the rivulets of water fall down his face. His eyes were red. Perhaps tears were mixed in with those water droplets.

"I promise I'll be careful," I whispered.

"You'd better be."

"I will."

"Good, because, Frankie," he said, shifting so we were only inches apart. For a moment I wondered if he would kiss me—wishful thinking. He'd never once acted like he saw me as more than a friend. Why start now? "If you don't hurry back," he continued, "I won't have anyone to do this with..."

My breath caught. "Do what?"

He picked me up and threw me across the water.

I shrieked, dunking under the surface. Everything stilled to weightlessness for the briefest of moments. I pushed my legs to swim hard and broke through the surface with a laugh. *Tristan was going down!*

"Oh, you think you're so smart, don't you?" I swam toward him.

"I know I am." He winked and took off in the other direction. There was no hope in catching up, Tristan was way too athletic, but knowing him, he'd pretend to have a leg cramp and let me get my revenge anyway.

He was my best friend, and just for today, we'd swim, we'd play, and we would pretend that nothing between us could ever change.

AFTERWORD

Thank you so much for reading my book. If you enjoyed it, please tell your friends and write a little review on Amazon and/or Goodreads. It makes all the difference! You can find all four full-length books of the The Color Alchemist series in print, audio, and ebook, plus my other series, by checking out my author profile on Amazon or my website. I hope you do.

XOXO,

Nina Walker

THANK YOU

Thank you to everyone who's supported and assisted in the creation of this short prequel novel. It's been loads of fun to write Tristan's history in Among Shadows. Be sure to read all four full-length novels in The Color Alchemist series for the complete story.

I especially want to thank Travis Walker, my husband, who is incredibly supportive of me and was my inspiration for Tristan. I don't want to spoil anything for the later books, so that's all I'll say for now about that. I want to thank Molly Phipps for her wonderful cover design. Kate Foster for her mad editing skills. Kate Anderson, Ailene Kubricky, and Sarah Mostaghel for being awesome proofreaders. The entire crew of authors and assistants in the Cursed Lands Boxset where this was first published. And finally, all the readers who continue to make this gig possible for me. From the bottom of my heart, thank you all so much!

ABOUT THE AUTHOR

Nina Walker is a USA Today and Amazon Top 100 Bestselling author. She lives near the beautiful red mountains of southern Utah with her family. She writes across multiple YA genres and loves metaphysical magic systems, forbidden love interests, and unexpected plot twists. She takes pride in publishing books that both teens and adults can enjoy.

Learn more at www.ninawalkerbooks.com or follow her shenanigans on Instagram @ninabelievesinmagic